I0788826

Pearls
of
Salt
and
Sacrifice

Pearls of Salt and Sacrifice

Sacrificed Hearts

Everly Haywood

PEARLS OF SALT AND SACRIFICE

This one is for my readers.

I love you guys!

CHAPTER ONE

Desolate and abandoned, Black Rock Island cut out of the sea like a jagged obsidian blade. Princess Reva Morrigan stood on the only point of access on the long, winding strip of land, her boots sinking into the white sand, stark against the dark rocks that fringed the beach.

While this tiny strip of rock and sand in the middle of the South Oloren Sea was hardly the place one might expect to hold important negotiations, beggars couldn't be choosers…and neither could princesses who hoped to create new trade routes and save their people from slow starvation.

These treaties wouldn't come without a price. Bile rose in the back of Reva's throat.

How much would she have to sacrifice to put food in the bellies of her people?

She turned from the beach to gaze out over the sea where three ships moored in the deeper waters. It had taken the *Perseus* two days to travel from Etthan to Black Rock, but the two other ships had needed to journey much farther. The *Andromeda* out of Seriposa had traveled at least four days, and Prince Felix and the *Endellion* had been at sea for several weeks.

The rowboat bearing the Destan prince and his political emissaries bobbed against the waves as the sailors strove toward shore. They were the last to arrive.

"A fine sight, is it not, Princess?" A voice smooth as silk whispered in her ear.

She flipped a hand over her shoulder to shoo the speaker away.

"Yes," she said, filling her tone with every drip of sarcasm she possessed. "It's a lovely day, for sure."

She gestured at the low, gray sky and refused to shiver in the cool wind that whipped from the north. She wore a sturdy long coat over her day dress, with trousers hidden underneath that, but the northern breeze still cut through her clothing.

"I meant the *Andromeda*, poppet." Captain Rency shifted to whisper in her other ear.

His warm breath stirred her unruly hair and tickled her cheek. She shot him a quelling look. "Keep your distance, Rency. Your invitation can be revoked."

A pair of blue-black eyes peered into her own. Captain Rency of the *Andromeda* merely smirked, his thin lips curving in just the right way to deepen the dimple in his left cheek. Only one. The cad.

When combined with his meticulous goatee, the dimple gave him an adorable, lopsided appearance that shouldn't be allowed in pirate captains, even if they happened to be on friendly terms with the Crown Princess. Rency and Reva had been working together for a while to find new food sources for Etthan. Against her better judgment, she'd almost grown fond of the scoundrel.

"Ah, you wouldn't do that to me, Reva. Not when I worked so hard to get here."

"*Princess* Reva, if you please. You haven't earned the privilege to be so informal, Rency."

Besides, he wasn't here based on his merit. He was here because he'd proven useful in bringing small loads of food to Etthan…at an outrageous price, too. It wasn't enough by far, but it kept a few people from starving. At first, she'd hoped Rency would be the answer to her food storage problems…but when he hadn't been able to supply enough food, she'd been forced to turn her gaze to fatter, wealthier fish.

"*Captain* Rency," he corrected as he locked his hands behind his back and rocked back and forth on the heels of his boots. "If we're going to get our knickers in a twist about *formalities*."

They stared at one another, neither willing to concede defeat first.

"I shouldn't be surprised to learn that pirates *can* get their knickers in twists," Reva said as the rowboat moved closer to the shore. "After all, you lot barely manage to keep your shirts on." She let her gaze drift pointedly to his partially buttoned tunic.

He'd missed more buttons than he'd managed to utilize—a strategic oversight during his morning ablutions.

Naturally.

Rency's dark eyes flickered with amusement. "Merchant sailor, lass. You've wounded me. Pirate, indeed."

He had the audacity to look offended.

She would have liked to arrest him then and there simply for being annoying; but, curse his black heart, she needed him to secure her contract with Prince Felix. The best routes to Desta went through Rency's territory. Without his leave to pass through the seas around Seriposa…well, any alliance with the Destans would do her no good if her boats were waylaid by pirates and stripped down to the timbers.

Several of his shady *merchant sailors* loitered nearby at that very moment, their clothing wrinkled and faces poorly scrubbed. A skinny fellow with an eyepatch even had his pinky finger in his ear.

Such a reputable-looking lot.

"Don't stand like that, Reva."

Her stepmother's voice sliced between them as Lady Cassandra approached from the striped canopy the sailors had constructed for her along the edge of the beach. She wore a frivolous, wine-red dress with puffed sleeves and a fitted bodice that showed off her ridiculously thin frame and ample assets.

"You look like a cabin boy," Cassandra said. "Feet together now. Hands folded."

When Reva didn't move, Cassandra swatted the girl's hand with a folded whale bone fan.

It stung.

But Reva refused to respond with anything more than a frown.

"Oh, please. At least I'm wearing a dress. I'd make one ridiculous-looking cabin boy in this ensemble."

"If that can even be called a *dress*." Cassandra's voice dripped with displeasure. "Would it have hurt you to wear something pretty? With a little color?"

"Yes, it would have hurt me," Reva said with thinly veiled impatience. "I'm here to bargain with Desta, not throw myself at their mercy or dither behind a fan. This is a mission of necessity, and I'm dressed to suit the occasion."

"People are hungry." Rency's quiet words held an unusual note of genuineness.

Reva slanted a look in his direction. "Very hungry. This blight has gone on for far too long."

"It's strange—" Rency stroked his jaw with a thoughtful air. "—that Etthan is the only island that seems to be affected. Is it not?"

Reva ground her teeth together. "Yes, yes, it's strange."

"One might think," the pirate captain said, his gaze holding Reva's, "that your island is cursed."

Cassandra fell prey to a sudden fit of coughing. Rency thumped her on the back and earned himself a foul look as repayment for his assistance.

"Don't be ridiculous," Cassandra said as she fanned herself violently. "Cursed, indeed. That's complete nonsense."

"I wouldn't be so sure." Rency locked his hands behind his back and watched the boat's progress. "Curses come in many shapes and forms."

Dread coiled in Reva's stomach. "I've considered almost every cause imaginable and must confess a curse never occurred to me."

"Of course not!" Her stepmother grumbled under her breath.

Reva, while not given to flights of fantasy as a general rule, wondered if Rency's suspicion held any merit. The blight *was* something no one had seen before, a festering sort of disease that caused the roots of their crops to rot. By the time the leaves began to turn black, notifying the farmers of an issue, it was already too late. The harvest was beyond saving.

Unaware of her grim train of thought, Cassandra snapped open her fan and waved it about with irritated flare. "It's more likely the sea elves did something to the island, just out of spite."

Reva suppressed an impatient sigh. She would never understand her stepmother's deep-rooted hatred of the elves. "I don't find that any more likely than cursing—we haven't seen or heard of the elves in my lifetime."

"Doesn't mean they aren't out there," Cassandra said grimly, two bright spots of color inflaming her cheeks.

Reva wished for the hundredth time that she understood the regent better. Her stepmother had always been aloof and private about her life prior to her short-lived marriage to Reva's father. His death a year after marriage to Cassandra had stunned everyone, Reva most of all. To be left alone in the world at the age of fourteen with only a stepmother she barely knew acting as regent until Reva turned eighteen…

Tears pricked at the back of Reva's eyes. Three years later, and the pain still felt as fresh as it had the day they laid her father to rest at sea.

"But you're right, of course," Cassandra was saying. "We're here to find genuinely helpful solutions. And, regardless, Reva, you're *still* dressed to wake the dead. You'll hardly snag Prince Felix's eye while wearing *that*."

"I'm not here to catch his *eye*." Reva repositioned at last and stood as her stepmother suggested, in a ladylike pose with hands folded in front of her. "I'm here to secure his trade routes."

She spoke the words with sickly-sweet innocence and batted her eyelashes at Cassandra, who glared and fanned herself with a fury.

"It's easier to catch flies with honey," Rency said.

A muscle twitched in Reva's cheek, but she refused to respond to the remark.

"Such wisdom in a fair maiden," Rency said. He splayed a hand over his chest and smiled at Cassandra as if she'd sprouted angelic wings along with her eternal wisdom. "I know *I'm* easier to catch with honey." His gaze cut back to Reva's. "I'm fond of green, myself. The emerald kind, especially if it's paired with dark, lovely skin and ebony tresses—"

Reva swatted his hand away when he tried to trail the back of a calloused finger down her cheek. "Touch me with that finger, Rency, and it will never leave this beach."

His eyes glinted with dastardly humor as Cassandra gasped an appalled, "Really, Reva! Such language."

"Dear me," Rency said and hugged his threatened appendage to his chest. "You'd actually cut off my fingers because I couldn't resist the allure of your flawless complexion?"

"I can remove your tongue too, pirate. That silver bit of your anatomy might sweeten the pot."

"Reva! That will do!" Cassandra's voice had grown more sour, if that were possible. "You sound like a cannibal! What if Prince Felix hears you? They're pulling up on the shore now."

True enough, the sailors from the *Endellion* had finally beached the rowboat and were assisting the broad— shouldered prince of Desta onto firm ground. He looked a little green around the gills, and she wondered if he had no taste for the sea. His soft brown curls plastered against his forehead, heavy with spray. The sickly pallor of skin contrasted starkly with the sunburn blazing across his nose and cheeks.

This one didn't often leave his plush throne.

Pity that.

She loved a rolling deck beneath her feet and the cutting ocean wind in her hair. It would have been easier to bargain with a man she understood, but Prince Felix…she doubted they had anything in common.

The prince took time to straighten his jacket and brush off his sleeves before slogging through the white sand toward Reva, two gentlemen in heavy coats and cravats stumbling at his heels. One of them clutched a satchel to his chest and shot nervous looks at Rency's pirate entourage.

The skinny fellow with the eyepatch grinned and waved a greeting that made the advisor squeak and shuffle faster to keep up with Prince Felix.

"Isn't he a fine dandy?" Rency whispered as he planted himself at her elbow, like he belonged there. "Not one of them looks like they could keep their footing in a stiff wind."

Reva elbowed him and took a small step to the side. "Shut up!"

Prince Felix drew up in front of her and offered a stiff bow. "Princess Reva. What a dastardly place for a meeting. I suggest we sojourn to the *Endellion* for negotiations."

She opened and closed her mouth several times. *Good morning to you, too.* But she finally managed to plaster a smile on her face. "While a lovely idea, I would prefer to remain on the beach. Neutral ground, as it were."

He swore like a sailor. Reva arched an eyebrow as Rency burst into choking laughter.

"*Such language.*" Cassandra flipped her fan toward the prince. "Really, Felix, you must control your tongue in the presence of ladies."

"Apologies, Cassandra," Prince Felix said with a dip of his head.

He didn't sound remotely sorry, however.

Something in Reva's stomach tightened. When had her stepmother and Prince Felix come to use first names? She hadn't been aware that they'd ever had much contact, outside the occasional political gathering. Relations with

Desta had been strained for years. She flicked her gaze between the two of them, assessing this new revelation.

"Well, if you insist on doing this here," Cassandra said to Reva, a petulant curl to her lips, "I suggest we sojourn to the awning to get out of this horrid gale."

It's hardly strong enough to call wind. But Reva kept this remark to herself and fell into step behind the others, the dutiful princess. Rency strode alongside her, grinning as if someone had just handed him a chest of royal treasure.

"Is everything in order?" Cassandra asked Prince Felix.

Reva tore her annoyance from Rency and focused on the pair in front of her. They walked close together, Cassandra resting her hand lightly on Prince Felix's arm.

"Yes," the prince said tersely. "My father took some convincing, but in the end, he saw reason."

Reva parted her lips, keen to know what they'd been keeping from her, but something caused her tongue to stick to the roof of her mouth. She clamped her lips shut and decided to tread carefully. She couldn't risk negotiations going sour.

She could berate her stepmother later. Cassandra *was* still regent, for a few more short weeks. And while Reva had been gradually taking over duties with the help of her advisors for almost a year now…Cassandra still held a position of authority in Etthan.

One that would come to a screeching halt when Reva turned eighteen.

"They're thick as thieves, aren't they?" Rency whispered as Cassandra and Felix stepped beneath the shade of the canopy and made themselves comfortable on the cushions

Cassandra had artfully arranged around a fire pit ringed in black rocks. The flames flickered feebly in the breeze and cast little heat.

Reva sat across from them as Rency threw himself down beside her, stretching out his long legs and hooking one boot over the other. He laced his fingers behind his head and smiled inanely at them each in turn.

"Why is he here?" the prince asked, his eyes narrowed on Rency.

Cassandra coughed and folded her hands demurely in her lap. "The princess invited him."

Something burned inside Reva at the sight of her stepmother. She hated that pose—the downcast eyes and meekly folded hands.

Eyes were meant to flash and hands to grip swords.

Felix's brows drew together. Reva crossed her legs and smoothed her full skirt over them. Stiffening her spine, she braced for the discussions.

"He's necessary for negotiations," she said in her own defense. "The best shipping routes will take our ships past Seriposa. It only makes sense that we all agree to share the waterways."

"I'll agree to anything." Rency plucked a strand of dune grass from the ground and stuck it between his lips. "For a price."

A muscle ticked in Felix's temple, and Reva suspected he was suppressing the desire for more cursing.

"Fair payment will be dependent on your cooperation in negotiations." Reva shot him a quelling look.

Behave. Please.

But the way he smiled at her clearly indicated he had no intentions of behaving and every intention of bleeding her pockets dry.

Cassandra fluttered her fan once again, although why she needed to use it *in this galesome wind* was beyond Reva's understanding. She'd never taken the time to learn the language of fans.

Clear, plain words served a woman of any station better than the inane fluttering of whalebone and lace.

"Ignore him," Cassandra said with a pleading smile for Felix. "Let Reva have her merchant sailor if it makes her happy. Did you bring the contract?"

Contract?

Reva's spine stiffened. "How is there already a contract?"

Cassandra shot her a surprised look. "Pardon? I thought I discussed this with you. Prince Felix and I have arranged everything."

"What—What's in that contract?" Reva asked, dread expanding inside her like a storm over the ocean. "Why are we even here?"

"This meeting is just a formality," Cassandra said, her eyes narrowing as she stared back at Reva, "to seal the betrothal."

CHAPTER TWO

Bile rose in the back of Reva's throat.

"*What betrothal?*" she said between her teeth.

The fan fluttered beneath her stepmother's piercing blue eyes. "Why *yours*, of course, darling. Surely you didn't think you'd get trade routes for *nothing*. You and Prince Felix are to wed and secure our future. I'll stay in Etthan to manage things since you'll be much too busy in Desta to worry about the silly little details."

Her people were nothing more than silly little details?

Anxiety churned in Reva's stomach at the careless ease with which her stepmother spoke about Reva's future. Leave Etthan and her people?

Marry Prince Felix?

"I-I didn't agree to this." She managed to choke out the words at last.

Cassandra's blue eyes narrowed to icy slits, but her voice was merry when she replied, "Of course, you did, darling. You said you'd do anything to secure the trade agreements so our people wouldn't starve."

"Marriage wasn't on the table!"

"Now, child, don't be dramatic." Cassandra mouth pressed into a firm line. "Marriage was *always* on the table. You're a young woman coming of age. Surely you knew you'd be married sooner than later. Best it be to the dear prince of Desta who can put food in the bellies of your citizens."

Reva bolted from her cushion. The anxiety in her gut flared to full—blown panic as she kicked Rency's thigh in her haste to escape the awning. She strode across the beach, clutching her skirts about her knees, not caring that she'd exposed her trousers.

She'd known these negotiations would come at a cost. She should have been prepared for this.

But she'd expected to empty what little remained in the coffers, not sell her soul…or share her bed.

Squeaking sand indicated someone had followed her across the white sand.

"Reva!" Cassandra said, her voice biting. The older woman caught hold of Reva's elbow and halted her. "Pull yourself together, at once!"

Reva resisted and tried to wrestle her arm free, but Cassandra yanked her so close she could see the flecks of black in her stepmother's irises.

"I demand you return and apologize. The prince has come a very long way to accept your hand. How dare you throw his offer in his face?"

Reva jerked against the fingers digging into her forearm.

"How dare I? How dare *you*! You deliberately hid this from me because you knew I wouldn't agree to it! If you're so keen on a marriage alliance with Desta, then you can marry Prince Felix!"

"Don't be ridiculous. I'm in mourning."

"You haven't been in mourning for years." Reva raked the older woman with a fiery glare. "You're as cold as a fish, and just as slippery. You planned this. You planned all of this. You've always wanted control of Etthan, and I was the only thing standing in your way. Do you think you can marry me off to a third son and take my kingdom from me?"

More boots squeaked against sand. At last, Cassandra released her hold on Reva and allowed her to yank free and step away. Rency and the prince strode toward them, the wind blowing their hair about their faces.

Rency stopped abruptly and shielded his eyes with a hand. He looked not at them but over the waves lapping hungrily upon the white sands. Reva followed the direction of his gaze. What had captured his attention? He wasn't one to ignore drama unfolding around him.

There. Something dark rose out of the waves. A porpoise arching out of the waters?

But no, the thing in the water didn't possess the sleek shape of a sea creature, but rather a head and shoulders and torso of a man. Only a couple yards from shore, the man shook his head and tossed dark, clinging locks out of his face. He wore a sea-green tunic secured by leather belt, straps, and greaves. Armor capped each shoulder.

He strode toward the shore, driving through the waves as if they were nothing to him.

The prince of Desta swore once again. "Is that—" But he broke off abruptly as the stranger stepped onto the beach and headed for them, his bare feet leaving divots in the sand.

The man stopped in front of Reva. and she gaped, openmouthed, as she took in the soaked figure standing before her: broad shoulders, a chin darkened with stubble, long dark hair, and…pointed ears.

"You're not welcome here, elf," Cassandra said between her teeth.

The venom in her voice tore Reva's gaze from the stranger and to the red—faced woman standing beside her. Once again Reva wished she understood the cause of Cassandra's long—standing hatred of the elves. Knowing would have been useful at a time like this.

Their unexpected guest cleared his throat, and Reva returned her attention to him as he drew himself up taller.

"My name is Jareth Elesti, Prince of Argos," he said, the words resonating like distant thunder across the ocean. "I heard that Princess Reva is seeking an alliance, and I am here to add my name for consideration."

Sand and pearls! Reva's back stiffened as she reared her head back. "Consideration for *what?*"

The elf cocked his head to one side and held her captive with a stare so intense she couldn't have looked away had she wanted to. "For the right to request your hand in marriage and seal a treaty between our peoples."

While Rency threw back his head and howled with laughter, Reva felt...*nothing*. Her thoughts struggled to make sense of the elf's words. What made him think he could climb out of the sea after decades of silence and request a marriage alliance? It had been so long since she'd heard any news of the elves, she'd nearly forgotten about them beneath the waters of the South Oloren.

The more she thought about it, the more her shock gave way to confusion and irritation.

"How did *you* hear about this?" Cassandra asked dubiously, voicing Reva's own misgivings.

Considering she'd managed to keep these plans a secret even from her own stepdaughter, Reva couldn't blame her and wanted to know the answer to the question herself.

"I have my ways." The elf hesitated, but after a faltering moment he straightened his shoulders and lifted his chin. "We keep our distance from your people, but that doesn't mean we don't pay attention to the events above us."

Cassandra's nostrils flared and she took a step toward the elf, shaking her fan like a weapon. "You've been *spying.*"

"Of course, he's been spying. Everyone is always spying on everyone else," Rency said. "You can't expect the elves to behave any differently than the rest of us."

"I—I don't spy!" Cassandra snapped open her fan and waved it violently.

Reva parted her lips to try to redirect the conversation, but a sudden rumble shook the foundations of the island beneath their feet. Reva staggered and spread her arms wide, searching for the source of the disturbance as the others also struggled to keep their solid footing.

Screams tore across the waters. Her eyes clasped on the prince's flagship, moored in the bay. While the *Andromeda* and Reva's ship, the *Perseus*, sat peacefully in the sea, Felix's ship rocked precariously side to side, as if bucked by an invisible wind.

Then, with a roar that could wake the dead, a fireball engulfed the *Endellion* in hellish flames.

Flames licked at the ship's timbers. A railing gave way and sent a cannon hurtling into the sea with a tremendous splash. Screams, hoarse cries, and gargles of pain filled the air in a horrific cacophony.

"Sand and sharks, what's happening there?" Rency shouted.

But Reva couldn't tear her gaze from the desecrated vessel. A part of her brain couldn't quite make sense of what had happened, but then the truth hit her like a punch to the gut.

People are dying.

Figures, some of them with flames devouring their clothing, jumped into the ocean in an effort to quench the blaze.

Rency hollered to his men who were on the beach. "Gather round, lads! They'll need our help!"

Reva stumbled forward to assist but paused when she skidded past the prince of Destan. The one person who should have been dashing into the sea to aid his crew still stood with mouth hanging open.

"My prince!" One of his advisors tugged at his sleeve. "My prince! The crew needs our assistance!"

Still, Felix simply stood there, seemingly incapable of movement.

That told Reva all she needed to know about this man her stepmother had arranged for her to marry. If he could not even be counted upon to act for the good of his own ship and crew, how could she depend on him to care for a wife? For future offspring? For her kingdom?

Shaking, Reva fumbled with the ties on the back of her overdress, ignoring her stepmother's outraged gasp.

"Reva! What are you *doing*—"

"There are people dying, Cassandra!" Reva yanked up her skirt so that she could peel the dress over her head. "I'm going to help, and I can't do it in this thing."

In her haste, however, she hadn't loosened the ties enough and the dress caught halfway through her disrobing. With the skirt over her head, blinding her, and her arms still caught in the elbow—length sleeves…

Drat and blast!

"Perhaps I can be of assistance."

A low voice spoke from beyond the veil of fabric. Hands tugged at the sands—blighted dress as she struggled furiously to free herself. At last, it loosened and released her.

The elf blinked at her, holding her dress in both hands with a strange look on his face. Two bright spots of color slowly warmed his high cheekbones.

She couldn't say she blamed him for being embarrassed: under any other circumstances, she would have been properly mortified. But there wasn't time for it here.

"If you want to be of assistance," she said, her words clipped, "do something about the *Endellion*!"

He held her gaze for a fraction of a moment then offered a nod.

She lifted her arm, signaling Captain Dren of the *Perseus* who waited on the shore near the two dinghies that had brought Reva and her companions to shore. "Let's go!" she cried. "Longboats in the water. Offer what help we can!"

Rency and his crew had already boarded their own longboat and pushed free of the shore. As Reva dashed across white sand in her sleeveless tunic and trousers, she heard Felix shout after her, "What if there are more explosions?"

Despite her irritation at Felix, it was not a stupid question. However, could they simply leave these suffering people to die without trying to rescue them?

"Do what you want!" she shouted over her shoulder. "I'm going to help!"

"My prince—" She heard Felix's advisor insist again, and then nothing else.

Reva didn't wait to see what he would decide to do. For her part, she'd lost all respect for a man who could let his ship burn, immobilized by fear for his own safety. Ironically, she was far more impressed by the mouthy Captain Rency who rowed alongside his men to reach the survivors.

As she kicked off her own boots and splashed into the cold waters of the South Oloren, she only hoped they'd be in time to save the crew.

A young woman with a scarlet bandana tied over her hair, held out a hand to help Reva scramble into the dinghy. Isla, the first mate of the *Perseus* and a personal friend to

Reva, made room on the bench beside her so Reva could sit. The prince of the elves eased into the water beside them. He observed Reva with sober eyes, whose color shifted between green and blue like the water itself.

"I will call for help," he said.

With that, he dove into the waves and vanished. His bare feet flashed briefly, and then he was gone. Reva barely had time to admire the supernatural grace with which he disappeared into the ocean swells before she followed Rency's example and took up an oar.

Her crew had already dipped wooden paddles into the water, working without having to be ordered.

Reva's muscles strained as she fell into a rhythm that sent the small boat plunging over the waves. As they approached the burning ship, she sucked in a gasp of horror. The hull of the *Endellion* had become a withered, blasted, blackened thing.

And then there were the bodies up ahead...

Reva didn't want to look as they drew closer. Several lifeless forms bobbed in the waves with scorched clothing, blistered skin, and singed hair. Survivors screamed in agony. The sight and sounds were enough to make her sick, but she gripped the oars and pulled along with the crew of the *Perseus* as they rowed straight into the mayhem.

CHAPTER THREE

Tears burned the backs of Reva's eyes, but she couldn't give vent to them now. Tears would help no one here.

Rency's longboat drifted close to hers. His men had already hauled one victim aboard and were gathering a second.

"Where should we take the wounded?" Rency asked over the splash of waves against their boats and the crackling roar of fire.

"Take them to the *Perseus*!" she shouted back. "Our ship's medic will have supplies on board."

Rency flicked two fingers off his forehead to acknowledge her command, and Reva's thoughts became consumed with the reality of hunting for wounded sailors and hauling them on board the boat.

They bobbed alongside two sailors, one fighting to keep his fellow above the waves. Isla leaned beside her to help pull them out of the water. The boat dipped precariously as they heaved the more wounded of the two sailors over the side.

"Hurry!" The other sailor disappeared beneath a swell. He reappeared, sputtering, and flailed back toward the boat. "Sharks!"

Reva's heart gave a horrified lurch. She scanned the waves around them, searching for signs of predators being drawn to the blood.

Sure enough, at least two fins sliced through the waves. One of them angled straight toward them.

Shouting, Reva caught the Destan sailor by the back of his tunic and yanked hard. He kicked uselessly until several more pairs of hands reached around Reva to help. The shark fin raced toward them, only a couple of yards away.

With a final heave, they managed to pull the sailor out of the sea just as the shark disappeared beneath the boat.

The predator's sleek body bumped the bottom of their craft as he swept past them.

"That was close," Isla said in Reva's ear, panting from exertion.

"As if fire and drowning weren't bad enough." Reva met Isla's piercing gaze. "Now we must contend with sharks, too."

The first mate grimaced in reply as she reached for an oar.

They fetched another sailor from the water, a boy too young to have left home, half—blinded by blood flowing from a gash on his head.

Reva eased the trembling lad down in the bottom of the boat. Her undershirt clung to her skin, soaked with sweat and sea water. "How many more can we carry before we risk swamping the dinghy?"

"I would suggest only two more, Your Highness," said a sailor from the prow.

As they forged onward, Reva experienced a stab of brutal despair.

They would never be able to pull everyone from the water before the sharks found them. And yet what good would their help be if they overloaded their boat and sank it?

"Hopefully the sea elf brings help," Reva said to Isla as they rowed over a swell.

The dinghy lifted and dropped with a sucking lurch.

"Did he say he would?"

Reva nodded and set her mouth in a grim line. "Let's hope he's true to his word."

They fetched two more sailors from the water and turned toward the *Perseus*. Unable to carry any more, they rowed alongside the hull of the ship and transferred the wounded to the deck using ropes and a six-foot-long board that served as a stretcher.

Something broke the surface beside Reva. Swallowing a cry of alarm, she stared down into Jareth's face. He caught hold of the side of the boat and peered up at her, his dark hair plastered against his forehead and cheeks.

"I've ordered my hunters to take care of the sharks," he said, breathing heavily as water streamed down his face. "We're trying to create a perimeter so you can focus on the survivors."

"Thank you." She didn't know what else to say.

Jareth held her gaze for a moment longer and then released his grip. Inhaling deeply, he bobbed up and then disappeared into the waves without a sound.

He did not reappear.

"I believe he has stayed true to his word," Isla said with a wry laugh.

"I suppose he has," Reva said, wondering how Isla could find humor at a time like this.

However, Isla had been at sea since she was thirteen years old and had likely seen every tragic, ugly, awful thing the ocean had to offer. She was as weathered and seasoned as any sailor. Yet, beneath her gruff surface, was a heart that tolerated no cruelty and longed for justice.

The older girl was the closest thing to a role model and best friend Reva had ever had.

With the assistance of the sea elves, rescue efforts picked up speed. The elves swam to the victims faster than the boats could row and kept them afloat until they could be fetched from the water. And true to Jareth's word, when Reva scanned the ocean around them, she saw nary a shark fin.

A strange patch of darkness floating on the surface of the water caught her eye.

"Over there!"

Reva pointed, directing Isla and the other crewmates in her longboat. Isla nodded, and they set to rowing vigorously toward the blackened hull of Felix's ship. As they rowed closer, the acrid smoke burned her eyes and throat. Reva pressed her arm over her face and blinked away stinging tears. She searched the water for any sign of sailors that the sea elves might have missed. She spotted only debris from the *Endellion*, most still sputtering with flame.

And the strange black substance on the surface.

Blood?

No, not blood. There was far too much of it. Also, it was black—with the darkness of ink rather than red.

"Do you think the powder magazine exploded?" Isla asked as she pulled gently on the oar to try to keep the dinghy in place.

Reva dipped her fingers into the substance and examined it more closely. "I don't know. What do you think of this?"

Isla leaned forward for a better look. "Looks like oil of some sort."

"But then why didn't it burn?"

Before Isla could respond, a shout from a nearby sea elf caught their attention.

"I need help," the female elf shouted.

The sailor, clearly in great pain, flailed so violently that the sea elf struggled to keep his head above water.

"Over there first," Reva said.

The sailors drew alongside the elf. Isla and Reva leaned over to heave the wounded sailor aboard the longboat. He lay wailing in agony in the bottom of the boat, half his face drenched in blood. And his right shoulder…Reva couldn't even look at the carnage.

They rowed to the *Perseus* to unload the survivors using the plank and ropes. Albus, the ship's powder monkey and mascot of sorts, climbed down to help. As they secured their last victim to the plank, the sailor screamed in agony.

"Oy." Isla detained Albus who lingered on the bottom rung of the ladder once the last wounded victim had been lifted up.

"Aye, ma'am?" The boy, barely more than twelve years old, clung to the side of the ship like a seasoned sailor.

"What did you see before Prince Felix's ship burst into flames?" Isla asked. "Anything of note?"

Albus, clutching a rung with one hand, scratched his head with the other. "I was in the crow's nest," he said as a hint of color darkened his cheeks. "Trying to spy—er, watch—the proceedings on land."

Despite the gravity of the moment, Reva smiled at the lad's slip. He wouldn't have been able to hear anything from the ship, but she found it amusing he'd been determined to try. More than likely, the rest of the crew had put him up to it.

"I thought I saw something in the water. Ripples. Maybe a shadow. Then came the explosion. The fire."

"Did you see fins?"

Albus shook his head, his face wrinkling in concentration. "I don't think so? But maybe? It happened so fast, ma'am. The ripples, then the explosion. Might have been fins? I don't remember."

"Not very helpful," Reva said once the lad had been dismissed to scramble back on board the ship.

"We'll interrogate the crew—and the survivors," Isla said. "But if something was in the water…maybe this wasn't an accident."

"You're thinking of the elves?" Reva shielded her eyes with her hand and glanced about the area with a heavy sigh. "But then why are they helping?

"Your guess is as good as mine. The arrival of the sea elves was timely, though." Isla used her oar to push the dinghy away from the hull of the *Perseus* with the help of two other sailors who'd remained in the boat with them. "This would have taken far longer without them."

"Maybe it was just an accident—the powder magazine exploding, like you said. And maybe there wasn't anything in the water…just dolphins or a shark."

Isla didn't respond immediately, her shoulder muscles straining as she pulled on the oars. "I think all the wounded have been retrieved."

Bile rose to the back of Reva's throat once again, and she swallowed with difficulty.

"Yes. Should we return to the island, then? I suppose Prince Felix is due a status report."

"I suppose Prince Felix can kiss the soles of my boots," Isla snapped. "Why do we owe him a status report when he didn't care enough to come out and save his own people?"

Reva did not disagree. However, she knew better than to badmouth the prince in front of her crew, even one as high-ranking as Isla.

"After all, you were there," Isla said. "Captain Rency was there. And the sea elf. What's his name?"

"Jareth." Reva pulled hard at the oars. The tension in her shoulders increased at the reference to the elf prince. She hadn't taken the time to process his presence at Black Rock.

As she rowed, her thoughts now returned to his sudden arrival just before the attack on the *Endellion*. Coincidence? He and his people had been very helpful, so she found it hard to believe they'd been behind the attack. If so, why the pretense?

And why the desperate look in his startling blue-green eyes when he'd looked at her and announced he'd come seeking her hand in marriage?

"What's he doing here anyway?"

Reva hesitated and kept her eyes on the horizon behind them. She didn't really want to say the words out loud. "He *says* he is looking for a wife."

"A what?" Isla shot her a sharp look and then threw back her head and laughed. The sound echoed across the waves, harsh and unnatural after the horrifying sounds that had ricocheted over the waves that morning.

Sands and Pearls! Reva yanked harder at the oar, gritting her teeth. She'd come to Black Rock seeking trade routes...not suitors.

And now she had more suitors than she knew what to do with and the trade routes seemed...impossibly elusive.

"I'm sorry, Your Highness," Isla said, still grinning from ear to ear. "I don't suppose it's all that funny."

Reva tuned out the rest of Isla's diatribe until they had drawn up on the sandy shoal of Black Rock Island. Then she jumped into the surf and helped the crew drag the longboat high on the sand, out of the greedy tug of the tide.

"Thank you, Isla. And thanks to all of you." She nodded to each of the crew in turn. "You acted valiantly today."

They nodded, grim smiles on their weary faces.

Reva braced herself and marched toward Cassandra and Prince Felix who sat beneath the awning. From the corner of her eye, she spotted Captain Rency's longboat also drawing near the shore. Blast the fellow's poor timing. Reva hoped he'd be on his best behavior while she tried to smooth things over with Prince Felix.

But perhaps that was asking too much...he probably didn't even know what good behavior *was*.

Her fears were confirmed when he hopped out and, thanks to his longer legs, strode past her and reached the awning first.

"Felix! What, ho?" he asked as he stepped beneath the awning and threw himself down on a brocade cushion. "Where were you, man? Have you no care for your ship and crew?"

From where he sat on his own cushion, the guarded expression on Prince's Felix's face turned sour. "I dispatched my crew," he said. "And all of you went. There was no room for me in the longboat."

"We could've made room," Reva said under her breath. She remained on her feet beside Rency, so that she could kick him if the situation warranted it.

When Rency threw her a conspiratorial look, she responded with a faint smile. She had to admit that while she pretended to loathe, despise, and abominate the captain…he'd proven a steady ally to her the past couple of years. She just wished he would make more of an effort to behave. In many ways, he was like the annoying big brother she'd never had.

"Thanks to the sea elves," Reva continued, "we were able to save most of your crew. I counted six dead."

"I saw at least four," Rency added with an unpleasant curl to his mouth.

Cassandra took a step forward, her eyes hard as glass. "*Thanks to the sea elves?*" she asked bitterly. "I wager the sea elves are the *cause* of our trouble."

Reva braced herself to incur her stepmother's wrath. "Cassandra, there isn't any evidence of that. Unless you know something the rest of us do not?"

The older woman stabbed her fan toward the ocean and waved it around as if she were wielding a rapier. "I don't know anything that you don't. But if you'd paid attention in your history classes, you'd know the elves have always caused trouble for our people. They're dangerous. Their magic is dangerous. And I assure you I'm not the only one who holds this view." She snapped her fan toward Felix.

As if cued, the prince nodded. "I daresay you're right," he said. "It's no coincidence the elf shows up to challenge my suit for your hand and moments later *my ship blows up.* That's highly suspicious, if you ask me. Highly suspicious." His voice trailed off, and he shifted on his cushion as if uncomfortable.

"We didn't ask you," Rency said under his breath, and Reva clamped down on the urge to kick him in the shins.

While she didn't disagree with him, she didn't want him riling the prince either.

"I think there is more going on than meets the eye," Rency continued.

"Oh? Do tell." Cassandra's tone was snide. "You have suspicions? Come, let us hear them."

"I know better than to drop my anchor into troubled waters," Rency said, but flicked his gaze between Felix and Cassandra before looking to the sea. "If you want to blame the elf prince—who I personally witnessed trying to help the injured crew—you can take it up with him. Here he comes now."

Reva glanced toward the surf in the direction Rency had indicated. Sure enough, the waters parted and allowed the prince of the sea elves to stride unhindered from the gentle waves.

She'd spent her fair share of days at sea, but she'd never seen anyone *own* the water the way Jareth did. Isla, who'd been loitering on the beach, fell into Jareth's wake as he strode across the sand toward the awning.

"Welcome back, dear prince of the glittering sea." Rency leaped to his feet and performed a grand, sweeping bow thoroughly tinged with mockery. "We welcome your wisdom during these trying times."

Jareth halted just outside the awning,

"Do we?" Cassandra sniffed.

"Don't we?" Rency waved an arm toward Cassandra and Felix, who stood stiff and angry beside Cassandra. "I, for one, was most appreciative of the mermaid's—I mean mer*man's*—assistance."

When Isla pressed a hand over her mouth as if to suppress a laugh, Reva's lips twitched, but she schooled her expression. Prince Jareth offered a stilted smile, color darkening his cheeks.

"They don't have tails, Rency," Isla said in a cajoling whisper, loud enough for all to hear. "Mermaids have *tails.* Or have you no understanding of basic anatomy?"

Rency grinned and shot a wink in Isla's direction, and Reva suspected he probably had far more than a basic knowledge of that particular subject. *The skirt-chasing buffoon...*

"We prefer to be called elves," Jareth said. "We are sea elves. Not mer. Though I understand the distinction may be difficult for humans."

"Some would call you *sirens,*" Cassandra said, waving her fan viciously. "And they would say you murder sailors and drag them to the bottom of the ocean."

Jareth shot her a sharp look. "That is a term we stopped using many ages ago." His voice resonated and held a musical quality that Reva found soothing to the ear, like the crash of waves washing on shore or a stream burbling over rocks. "It's a *misleading* representation of my people. We do not drown sailors and try to avoid them."

"And yet," Cassandra said with an icy smile, "here you are."

"Yes." Jareth shifted his gaze to settle on Reva, his mouth turning down into a frown. "Here I am."

Her stomach churned unpleasantly as his intense blue eyes sought hers—he had this piercing way of looking at her, as if he could see through her, to her thoughts. It made her feel exposed...vulnerable. And she didn't like that.

She didn't like it one bit.

CHAPTER FOUR

Reva swallowed hard and squared her shoulders. "Yes, here you are," she said to redirect the conversation to safer grounds. "Here we all are. And it's time we stopped fighting with one another and started discussing real solutions."

"That's easy enough," Felix said with an injured sniff. "You can *hang* the elf for declaring war on Desta, and then you can take me home. We can get married there. And then we'll find some food for, you know, the hungry people."

Reva clenched her fingers at her sides, unable to believe what she was hearing. Her starving people were just an afterthought to him? Just 'the hungry people'? She'd never met a more despicable human being—and that was saying a lot, because she had the misfortune of knowing *Rency*.

"Splendid plan!" Cassandra said with all the chirpy enthusiasm of a bird at dawn.

"Absolutely not!" Reva choked out the words and spun to face her stepmother. "I won't be marrying *anyone,* especially a man who stood on the beach and watched his men drown! And especially not if the promised trade goods aren't already in my ports feeding *my people.*"

"Reva, you're overreacting again." Cassandra drew herself up, tapping her fan against the palm of her hand in a familiar gesture that told Reva they were ramping up for a royal squabble. "This has already been arranged."

"*I* am crown princess of Etthan." Reva said with deadly force. "And I made no such arrangements."

For that matter, she was as willing to consider Jareth's unexpected proposal of marriage as she was Felix's underhandedly arranged one. They both offered potential new avenues of trade. What could Jareth's people offer in the way of food?

Might they know how to fight the blight?

"Oh, darling," Cassandra said with a dramatic flourish of her fan. "I'm your regent. Of course I handled the betrothal details for you."

"A position you won't be holding for much longer, I assure you. I turn eighteen this year, and your position will be eliminated." The words exploded from her before she had a chance to think about the ramifications.

When Reva alluded to her impending coronation, all color drained from Cassandra's face, her eyes narrowing to angry slits. "You *will* marry for the good of your kingdom, Reva Morrigan."

"And I fully intend to." Reva clenched her fingers and then flexed them open against her damp trousers, searching for a calm she didn't feel. "One day. But *I* will be the one to determine which suitor will best provide for my people."

"You're not old enough to make such an important decision. You're going to marry Felix."

"Perhaps I will," Reva fired back, "but not today. And not without trade goods piled sky high in Etthan's ports."

"And it hasn't yet been determined that *Felix* is the best suitor," Rency said.

Silence fell over the awning as everyone shot him a startled look. While his posture was lazy, Reva recognized the glittering focus in his sharp gaze as he returned her piercing look.

"I, too, can offer trade with Etthan—and Seriposa isn't nearly as far away as Desta. My rates would be more reasonable, I'm sure."

Reva snorted. "I'm sorry, Rency, but while I appreciate your offer…and the help you've offered to present…Seriposa simply doesn't have the capacity to feed Etthan as well itself…and I can't in good conscience consider a proposal of marriage from a *pirate*."

"*Pirate* is such a nasty word." Rency's nostrils flared although he maintained his indolent smile. "And I'm not sure you entirely understand the meaning of it."

Cassandra raked Rency with a withering glare before shifting her attention back to Reva. "Thank the stars you have that much sense—it's as ludicrous as the offer from the *elf*. Reva, you don't have any idea who he is or what he's capable of. The elves *can't* be trusted."

"My people had nothing to do with the attack in the cove." Jareth's quiet voice wrapped around Reva's sorrow and soothed her.

She sniffed and lengthened her spine, holding her head high. She had duties to perform today. "Perhaps we should cease accusing one another," she said, trying to mask the exhaustion gnawing at her bones and tainting her words. The wind tugged at her damp clothing, her dark brown hair. Despite the warmth of the sun on her shoulders, a chill crept across her skin. "We've seen great tragedy today. Quarreling amongst ourselves helps no one."

"I will agree to no more quarreling," Prince Jareth said, his strange, ever—changing eyes locked onto her face. "I will merely state that my people are innocent. I came here today to enter into negotiations so that my people might return to the surface. We can offer knowledge of the sea, the best fishing grounds and better methods for catching fish…"

Reva swallowed with great difficulty. *So that my people can return to the surface?* What exactly did he mean by that? How many people did he want to bring with him if she were—by some wild chance—to take him up on his offer?

"Let there be a new era," he concluded, "a new camaraderie, between the realms of land and sea. We've lived apart for centuries…perhaps it is time to bring our people together again."

A stilted silence answered him. Jareth searched her face as if looking for something specific, but what did he want her to say? His proposed treaty came at the cost of her hand. A treaty sealed with marriage.

It all came back to this: Food for her hand. Treaties for her hand.

And what would happen if Reva refused his marriage proposal? Would the elves revert to their siren ways and haunt her trading ships?

Reva's hands shook as she pressed them against her thighs. Cassandra was right about one thing—she *wasn't* ready to make this kind of decision. Her gaze flickered between the petulant human prince and the enigmatic one from the sea—between two uncertain futures.

If she had to pick between them, she'd choose Jareth in a heartbeat. But she couldn't make such a decision based on personality. As the future queen of Etthan, she had to do what was best for her people.

Her personal preference could have no bearing.

That night, Reva found sleep difficult. Everyone had agreed to camp on Black Rock Island and continue talks in the morning. Cassandra had been so angry at Reva that she refused to eat dinner and instead sulked her way through the simple meal of rice and fish that the cook prepared for everyone else.

Was there a solution to this madness that didn't involve her agreeing to marry a stranger? Or her being forced to compromise what she believed was the best for her kingdom in order to feed her people?

Handing control of her kingdom to Cassandra was *not* what she wanted.

And yet…could she risk the future of her people on an unknown prince?

Reva rolled over on the thin mattress laid upon the sand. Every time she convinced her body to relax, a new concern seeped in and reignited her unease.

Frustrated, she flung an arm across her face. She might as well resign herself to the fact she wasn't going to sleep tonight—

A curious wriggling in the sand beneath her hip froze her mid thought. Gasping, she rolled to her knees, diving for the lantern in the corner of her tent. What had crawled into her tent? A snake from the rocks? Crab? Her skin prickled as she hastily lit the lantern. Crouching beside her bedroll, she lifted the lantern and search for—

Wriggling. In her pocket.

Shivering with revulsion, she set the lantern down and dug into her pocket, grabbing whatever had crawled into her trousers. She gave it a little fling. The squishy thing landed on her burlap pillow.

Rather than scuttle or slither away, the fist-sized creature drew in on itself as if it were scared, huddling on her pillow. Reva picked up the lantern for a closer look.

"By the pearls," she breathed, half-laughing at her own terror. It had too many arms to be a snake… Her unexpected bed fellow was nothing more than a tiny, rosy-pink, blobbish…

Kraken?

Reva sighed and set the lantern down on the ground.

"Where did you come from?" she asked as she eyed the baby kraken. "I really don't want you on my pillow."

As if responding to her calmer tone of voice, the kraken unfurled its tentacles and emitted an inquisitive squeak she *almost* found cute. Contrary to the fairy tales that liked to depict kraken as monstrous beings, most of the species were harmless creatures that seldom ventured out of the water. And when they did, they could only survive for a couple of days without returning to the sea.

"I don't know how you managed to find your way into my tent—or my pocket, for that matter," Reva said, "or why you thought it was a good idea, but you can't stay here. You're going to dry out."

The kraken scuttled forward an inch—then two inches—and blinked its black eyes at her.

Reva eyed it suspiciously. "Let's get you back to the sea," she said. "Your mother must be there, waiting for you."

Leaning over, she plucked the baby kraken up by a couple of its tentacles, stooped to climb out of her tent door, and darted barefoot across the sand toward the sea. The kraken curled a suction—cupped tentacle around her fingers. She shuddered and held it at arm's length, not appreciating the feel of its suction cups against her exposed skin.

"If you bite me," she said between clenched teeth.

The island was silent, save for the perpetual wash of waves against the shore and the crackling of the fire down the beach from her. Watchmen gathered about the flames, murmuring together.

Holding the blobby pink kraken before her, Reva ignored the watchmen, who hadn't yet noticed her, and walked toward the edge of the water. Felix's smoldering ship caught her eye. The fire's glow still permeated some of the timbers, and a wave of sadness washed over her as she considered the people who had lost their lives.

Would they ever learn if it was more than an accident? But if it wasn't, then who would do such a terrible thing?

"Here you go, little one." She stopped at the edge of the sea. The damp sand felt cool against her bare toes as she held out her arm and tried to release the kraken. "Time to go home."

It clung more tightly to her fingers and emitted a wee shriek.

"Oy! Let *go*—"

"Wait."

Reva jerked in response to the command from the darkness. She twisted her head to the right and watched Prince Jareth rising out of the water. Moonlight revealed his high cheekbones and cast his deep-set eyes into deeper shadow.

"What are you doing here?" she asked. "I thought you were asleep with everyone else. Are you watching me?"

Not a flicker of expression changed his face. "Yes," he said without any sign of shame. "And the sea."

"Watching for what?" she asked, a shiver rippling down her arms and legs.

He hesitated and looked over his shoulder, out into the cove. "I don't know," he said quietly.

There was something he wasn't telling her. Tentacles wiggling against her fingers reminded her why she'd come down to the water in the first place. "Oh. This fellow was in my tent. I don't suppose he's an acquaintance of yours, perhaps?"

Shaking her hand gently, she started to drop the creature into the waves.

"Actually, yes!" Jareth dove forward, catching the miniature kraken in his palm. He cradled it like he held something fragile and precious, and Reva suddenly wondered if she shouldn't have picked the blob up by its tentacles. Jareth tucked the creature away, safely in his own pocket.

"Forgive him," he said, sounding embarrassed as he rose to stand in front of her. "Calix doesn't always do as he's told."

Reva took a step backward, uncomfortable with his proximity. "It's alright. I don't always like to do what I'm told either. And he didn't cause any harm."

Silence wrapped around them but not the nice, comfy sort of silence between friends. This was awkward and strained, and made Reva want to retreat back to her tent as quickly as possible just so she didn't have to work at polite conversation.

"So." She cleared her throat and crossed her arms over her chest to ward off the night chill. "Why are you watching the cove? You said you didn't know what you were looking for?"

He didn't answer immediately but took the time to shove an escaping Calix back into his pocket. The kraken squeaked furiously. "I, uh, sense a disturbance in the water. Something…I can't explain. Something just doesn't feel right."

"What *does* it feel like?" Reva prodded, unable to keep her gaze from straying to the dark sea. Moonlight glinted off cresting waves all across the cove.

Once again he didn't answer right away. This time, however, he wasn't fussing with Calix but simply stared out at the waters he called home. "Something dangerous," he said finally. "I don't know what's out there, and that…"

"That worries you?"

"Yes." He half laughed and turned back to her. "I thought I knew most of the secrets of the Oloren…but this reminds me I still have much to learn."

She pursed her lips and considered her next words carefully. "So what do you think happened to the *Endellion?* Was it an accident? Or was it attacked?"

"You're asking me?" His voice lowered, his gaze searching hers.

"Um, yes, I believe I did." She arched one eyebrow and waited for him to answer more properly.

Jareth shifted his weight to the side but maintained eye contact. "I can't say for certain. But I don't think it was an accident. The sea doesn't lie…and it's telling me something is wrong. I can't explain it to you, not in words you would understand."

"Try."

"You're very direct." One corner of his mouth lifted in a lopsided smile. "Very well. It's not any one thing. It's the way the water tastes, the way the fish swim in unusual patterns. So many small things that would mean nothing by themselves, but when you add them together…"

They mean something. She finished his sentence in her head and rubbed her palms over her arms, a sensation of dread tightening in her stomach…a premonition of something *bad* headed their way.

Another awkward silence fell between them, and Reva stared at the cove and wondered what could be out there.

"You should try to sleep," Jareth said at last, his tone more subdued than it had been. "I want to go back into the cove. Continue my search to see if I've missed anything."

She nodded and shook off the clinging web of her own unease. Jareth didn't wait for a further response but slipped under the waves, disappearing into the dark water with a gentle splash.

Reva retraced her steps across the narrow beach and stooped to enter her tent, brushing off her feet before lying down on her mattress again. With any luck, no more sea creatures would be lurking in her clothing…

She draped an arm over her face and sighed as she tried to force her weary muscles to relax. But thoughts of the burning ship and screaming sailors filled her mind. Every time her thoughts strayed, she forced them away from the horrors she'd witnessed that day and tried instead to focus on her breathing—on tangible things like the lumpy mattress beneath her, the distant growl of waves against the shore, the scent of damp rock and salt and seaweed. She rolled onto her side with a weary sigh.

Something thumped outside her tent.

Reva's eyes flew open, and she held her breath. Was it the guard standing outside her tent? Had he dropped something?

Her fingers crept across the mattress toward the knife she'd place beside her pillow, the one she usually kept in her boot. She slid it from the sheath and stared at the tent flap a few feet away from her, barely able to make out details in the gloom.

Perhaps it was nothing, a mere trick of her tired mind.

But then the flap shifted and allowed a thin ray of moonlight to spill into the tent.

Her pulse thundered beneath her skin, her heart rate increasing with a jolt. Someone was coming into her tent whether she wanted them to or not. Should she scream for help or use the element of surprise to her own advantage?

More cold light flooded the tent as the flap pulled back to reveal a dark shadow beyond. The intruder moved, blocking out the moonlight as he stooped to enter the tent...

Reva shoved herself into a crouch, lifted her blade, and rasped, "Don't come any closer. *I'm armed.*"

CHAPTER FIVE

The intruder lunged, lifting a blade of his own. Reva grunted and threw herself out of the path of the dagger. Barely. She felt it slice through her clothing as she rolled across the mattress and came up with her own weapon raised high.

A dark shape loomed over her, hooded and cloaked. Reva sliced sideways with her blade, eliciting a hiss from her attacker as he dodged backward.

Then he swung toward her in retaliation. With little room to maneuver, Reva braced one hand against the ground and kicked out with her left leg, catching the attacker on the shins. He grunted and went down to one knee, the blade still held high over his head.

Reva dropped onto her back, tucked both knees to her chest, then kicked as hard as she could. Her bare feet caught him high on the chest, and the momentum of her strike flung him back through the tent opening.

"Intruder!" she screamed as loudly as she could. "I'm being attacked!"

Startled voices rose from around the beachside camp. Rather than wait to be attacked again, Reva scrambled to the left and dove beneath the side of the tent, worming her way in between two stakes. She wiggled over the sand and crouched low on the beach. Dagger clenched in her fingers, she eased to the edge of the tent and peered around.

A form lay motionless on the ground outside her tent, but no one else was in sight, the moonlight shining on an empty beach. She spun side to side, the hand that held her dagger trembling. From the south, dark shadows dashed from the direction of the fire pit, straight toward her.

Someone tried to murder me in my sleep!

Anger overran her fear as she searched for signs of the intruder, but other than the watchmen approaching there was nothing to see. Where had he gone?

She knelt beside the fallen guard and felt his throat. A pulse throbbed against her fingertips, and she breathed a sigh of relief.

Bobbing lanterns glinted in her eyes as three guards dashed toward her.

"Princess!" one of them called. "Princess Reva, is that you? What's wrong?"

"I'm alright." Reva stalked into the circle of lantern light. "But my guard's been hurt. Someone search my tent, please. There was an intruder." Her legs wobbled, but she was grateful her voice didn't quiver.

Two of the guards peeled off to obey—one kneeling beside his fallen comrade while the other ducked into her tent—while the third placed himself beside her.

"Reva, what's going on?" Lady Cassandra appeared from her own tent, belting her brocade robe about her body as she approached. Reva wondered how she'd managed to climb out of bed so quickly. "What have you done? What's all this horrible yelling?"

"What have *I* done?" Irritation flooded Reva like icy salt water through a crack in the hull of a ship. "Why do you blame *me*? I didn't attack myself in my own bed!"

"Reva, you're acting hysterical."

"You would, too, if you'd nearly been murdered!" Reva drew a breath.

She could not believe her stepmother was attempting to lay the blame for this nighttime disturbance on her! She took several deep breaths then explained to those gathered around her.

"I was in my tent trying to sleep when something startled me, and I saw my tent door opening. I grabbed my dagger, warning them to stop, but they tried to slash me anyway, and—"

"Reva, my love," her stepmother said, interrupting Reva's accounting of her ordeal, "this is a most fanciful story. Are you certain you didn't dream the entire matter?"

Reva's eyes narrowed. Why did Cassandra always dismiss her concerns? She'd always treated Reva like a helpless child who couldn't so much as pull on her own boots.

When someone grabbed Reva and spun her about, she instinctively lifted her dagger to defend herself. Rency's bearded face peered into hers, halting her hand moments before she drove the blade into him. He lowered his gaze to the dagger before meeting her gaze.

"Don't stab me, please," he said with a twist of his lips.

She tried to pull away as he ran his hands roughly down her arms. Pain flared just below her elbow, and she punched Rency in the stomach.

"Ow! That hurts."

Nonplussed, he caught her wrist and turned it skyward. Something slick coated her arm, the sight of it turning Reva's stomach.

"She's bleeding," Rency said in a cold voice, turning toward Cassandra. "Do you think she did *that* to herself? In her sleep?"

Cassandra folded her arms over her torso, pressing her lips together as Rency clasped Reva's hand and twisted the dagger from her tense fingers.

Fear shivered across her skin, but Rency merely sliced the hem of his own tunic before offering the dagger, hilt first, back to Reva. She took it with a suspicious glare but held still as he began to bandage her injured arm.

Reva lowered the dagger to her side, but she curled her fingers tightly around the hilt in case she needed it again. Footsteps squeaked in the sand moments before Felix appeared, rubbing his puffy eyes. "What's all the noise about?" he asked around a yawn.

"Reva was attacked," Rency explained.

"She—what?"

"Did anyone see anything?" Reva asked, looking at the three guards who'd been assigned the night watch. They looked at one another, then shook their heads.

"All was quiet, Your Highness. We didn't suspect anything was amiss until you shouted."

"Well, search the island," Cassandra said. "The attacker couldn't have gotten far. Where is that elf prince? I would wager he's behind this. First the *Endellion* and now my poor, helpless stepdaughter. He's trying to turn us against one another."

Poor, helpless *stepdaughter…who had chased her would-be-murderer away with her own blade…*

"Oh, please." Reva pinched the bridge of her nose "Why are you blaming Prince Jareth? I don't think he had anything to do with this. I saw him shortly before the attack, and he was headed out into the cove to keep watch. If he had plans to hurt me, he would have done it then when I was alone on the beach."

The instant the words left her mouth, she re—thought them. Her stepmother's eyebrows flew upward. "What were you doing consorting with that elf prince in the middle of the night?" Cassandra asked. "Unchaperoned?"

"My, my, this is most distressing," Rency said, rolling his eyes pointedly. He locked gazes with Reva, his fingers still clasping her wrist. "How *could* you be so careless with your reputation? Think of your virtue."

"Oh, shut up." Reva yanked free of his hold, yelping at the flash of pain. "You're the last person on this island who should be worried about such a trivial matter as a reputation."

"I'm sure I don't know what you mean." He had the audacity to look affronted.

Black—hearted pirate, she longed to throw at him, but she pursed her lips and kept silent.

Rency dipped his head toward her, his voice a low murmur. "Perhaps we should have a private chat. I have thoughts about this debacle I'd like to discuss with you."

Reva arched her brow. "You have *thoughts* on the matter, do you? Anything you wish to say to me privately you can say before everyone else."

She had no desire to be alone with Rency right now. She wouldn't put it past him to try to steal kisses in the moonlight. The last thing she felt like doing at the moment was fending off the self—proclaimed leader of a miniscule island in the middle of nowhere.

"You still haven't answered my question," Cassandra said, pulling Reva's attention back to her. "Why were you meeting with the elf prince? I don't trust him, Reva. Furthermore, I forbid you to be anywhere near him or his kind!"

"His *kind*? Cassandra, do you even hear yourself?" Reva drew a breath, releasing it out her nose. "I was returning one of his pets that had wandered into my tent. I returned it, I came back to my bedroll, and the attack occurred a short while later. Why would he have waited until I returned to my bed before slitting my throat? Why not kill me on the beach when he had the chance?"

"Then who?" Felix blustered, inserting himself into the conversation yet again. "Who's behind this if not the elves? No one else profits from the failure of these negotiations. And it is *clear* someone doesn't want you to get your trade routes, Reva."

Reva said nothing because she didn't disagree with him. Her instincts whispered that the *Destans* had more to gain by removing her from the throne—seeing how they were so chummy with Cassandra—but why would Felix destroy his own ship?

"I don't know," she said around a wave of weariness. "I'm going back to bed. However," she said, with a significant glance at everyone gathered around her, "If this should occur again, I will defend myself. *Again.* I am no helpless princess."

She directed that last remark at her stepmother.

Then she darted around Felix and ducked back to her tent. Pulling the flaps together was not nearly as satisfying as slamming a door might have been, but shutting them all out was the only defense she had against the flood of emotions building inside her.

"Reva…" Cassandra's irritated voice rose from behind the tent canvas.

"Good night, stepmother!"

Her pulse thundered in her ears as she braced herself for a quarrel with her only living relative. But shuffling feet in the sand suggested everyone was moving away. She caught snatches of conversation, such as: *"Stand guard…Watch her closer…"*

She sat down on her mattress, facing the tent flap, and willed her taut muscles to unwind. Tears burned behind her eyes as the adrenaline faded and left her feeling weak and sick. The shadow of a guard pacing outside her tent brought her no comfort.

She let herself cry because no one was watching. Wiping her cheeks with the back of her hand, she lay down facing the tent opening, clutching her dagger in her hand and wondered if she'd have to endure another attack tonight.

Could she trust her own guards? She wanted to because she'd known them most of her life.

She still didn't think Felix was capable of this. So who else did that leave?

Jareth, who could have killed her on the beach but hadn't? Or Rency, who had been her off and on ally for nearly two years now?

While he wasn't particularly likable, he'd never done anything to suggest he wished to harm her.

Annoy her half to death, yes—but harm her? No.

Who else did that leave? Cassandra? Reva swayed as exhaustion crept over her in pulsing waves. That wasn't an accusation she wanted to make without solid proof. While she had no love for her stepmother, she'd never seen her do anything that suggested she was more than a conniving courtier who wanted fancy gowns and jewels.

Her mind tumbled over the problem again and again until she grew too weary of trying to unscramble motives and fell asleep.

Something warm and damp pressed against her cheek. Reva's eyes snapped open, and she struggled to focus on the pink blob beside her face.

Yowling, she bolted into a seated position, grappling for the dagger beside her bedroll. Sunlight streamed through the crack in the tent opening.

"Sand and pearls!" she said to the baby kraken nestled on her pillow. "You horrible, rotten little beasty! You almost gave me a heart attack. What are you doing here?"

The tiny blob of tentacles and suction cups unfurled like a flower opening its velvety petals to the sun. Calix stretched his many arms and blinked his dark, pearl—shaped eyes. A sound reverberated from him, like…like…

"Are you *purring*?" Reva pushed her messy braid over her shoulder. "For crying out loud. Have you adopted me or something? Because I certainly didn't adopt *you.*"

In response, the tiny creature only purred louder and stretched a tentacle toward her. She hesitated and then offered a wary fingertip. Calix coiled his warm appendage around her pointer finger. Before she realized what he was up to, the kraken had begun to coil around her hand and was oozing up her arm, making sucking noises as he crawled across her skin.

"Oh no. Pearls, no! Yuck. Ew. Just…ew!" She tried to grab him, but the squishy feel of the kraken's body beneath her fingers nearly made her wretch. Squeezing her eyes closed and bracing for the most unpleasant experience of her life, she let it crawl up to her elbow and then over to her side. She peeked down as the kraken oozed his way into the pocket of her trousers, where he curled into a warm, vibrating ball.

Despite herself, Reva cracked a smile. "Well, I guess that isn't so bad. But don't get used to it, Blob. I'm giving you back to Prince Jareth the first chance I get, I promise you that."

Reva loosened her braided hair, brushed out the long, black tresses, then hastily re-plaited it into a tight braid that should stand up against the sun, wind, and sea. When she reached for clean clothing from her sea chest, her outstretched arm showed off the slashed sleeve and bloodied bandage from Rency's shirt—a visible reminder of last night's attack.

Reva shivered.

Reva pushed these thoughts away as she pulled a clean tunic and skirt from her travel pack. The skirt she'd chosen was one of her own design, with several straps and buckles to hoist the skirt up above her knees in the front, leaving her free for movement. It exposed her trousers and knee-high boots gloriously.

Cassandra *hated* this skirt.

Reva grinned as she slipped her favorite pendant over her head—a gift from her father for her thirteenth birthday— and then reached for her earrings. She'd taken them off the night before, placing them in a tiny box she'd set on the ground next to her pack. The pearls—woven together with sea stones in a small, intricate knot—had once belonged to her mother.

"Where are they?" she asked, growing frustrated when she could find neither the box nor the earrings.

Exasperated, Reva sifted through everything in her tent, desperately searching for the tiny box. It had probably gotten tossed about during last night's attack. It seemed the most logical explanation, and yet, try as she might, she could not find the box or earrings.

A heavy sense of discouragement settled over her shoulders. Could the attack have been motivated by theft rather than murder? But who would go through so much trouble for such inexpensive earrings, whose value lay in sentiment not the gems it boasted?

Yet the jewelry was truly gone. She'd not brought many possessions on this trip—quite unlike Cassandra, with her multiple sea chests of all sizes—and Reva was certain she had searched everywhere within the confines of her tent.

Tears burned behind her eyes. Last night's attack, her lack of sleep, the emotion of losing such a prized possession…

She ran her hand beneath her nose and then wiped away her tears with trembling fingers. They were the only tears she had time for. She dried her face, squared her shoulders, and burst from the tent into the gray mist of early dawn. She lifted a calming hand to the watchman who sprang to his feet as she stalked past. He sank back on his heels beside the fire. She could almost feel his eyes following her as she strode toward the waves lapping against the sandy beach. At the edge of the water, she knelt, pulled Calix from her pocket despite his squeaks of protest, and prepared to slip the stowaway back into the sea.

"I'll take him, please."

Reva yelped and toppled onto her backside on the damp sand. Clinging to the kraken in one hand, she braced herself against the ground with the other, her fingers sinking into the sand.

Prince Jareth stared down at her, his dark hair dripping as if he'd just emerged from the sea. His tall body, clad in dark green and black armor, contrasted starkly with the white mist wafting from the ocean he called home.

Her tongue stuck to the roof of her mouth. There was something so ethereal about him. Something otherworldly. Mysterious. She couldn't help but wonder what his underwater kingdom must be like.

The wonders it must hold.

Wonders human eyes had never seen.

A wayward thought skittered across her thoughts—what would her life be like if she married a prince of the sea? With Felix, she saw aloof indifference. Cold throne rooms and long meetings where she constantly had to fight for her right to her own kingdom.

But what if she were to accept Jareth's offer? *Could* she even accept it? Where would they live? And how?

That path lay shrouded in shadows and mist. Unknown. Uncertain.

And yet…she could almost feel the roll of a deck beneath her feet, the sea wind in her hair, a sensation of freedom and belonging wrapping around her…

Jareth stretched a hand toward her, and she hissed between her teeth and scuttled backward. He froze, sea-green eyes confused. "I'm sorry," he said, brows pinching together above his nose. "I-I didn't mean to startle you. I just—I was hoping I could have my kraken back. Please."

"Oh." She waved the hand holding the creature in question. "You mean this kraken? The one that snuck into my tent *again* and made himself at home on my pillow?"

The sea elf's cheeks reddened like the skyline at sunset, and Reva found herself more convinced than ever that anyone who looked this *adorable* couldn't possibly be the villain in her story.

"Yes," he said as he cupped a hand over the back of his neck. "*That* kraken."

She tensed her thighs and heaved herself into a crouched position so she could rise to her feet. The prince stepped forward as she offered her hand and quirked a smile, reaching for the squirming pink creature. Calix squeaked and clung more tightly to Reva's fingers as Jareth tried to pry him free.

His fingers brushed over hers as he fought to disentangle the stubborn blob. Calix's suckers pulled and popped loose one by one.

The redness in Jareth's cheeks only deepened.

"This one must give you a lot of trouble," she said as Jareth finally slid the kraken's last tentacle from Reva's finger. A gentle popping noise announced when the last sucker released. She rubbed her hand, which tingled with a mild itchy sensation.

"You could say that." Jareth's fingers slid from hers, and a strange thrill passed through her core. Her gaze flew up to Jareth's. Had he felt it too?

He was staring at the kraken, not her. "Thank you," he said as he gently tucked the kraken away into one of his vest pockets. "Sometimes they're bound and determined to escape and go where they shouldn't."

"I see. Perhaps you should put buckles on your pockets." Reva pointed toward the pocket where the miniature kraken had gone.

"But I wouldn't want them to feel trapped," Jareth said, his gaze falling to his boots, which he scuffed in the sand, as if embarrassed. Seaweed twined around his boots, reminding her that he was no ordinary human, but a creature of both land and sea.

"That's noble of you." The wind teased a strand of hair out of her braid and flung it against her mouth. Impatiently, Reva swept it behind her ear. "Did you discover anything in the cove last night?"

A wrinkle formed between the elf's eyebrows. When he didn't answer, Reva exhaled slowly to mask her frustration.

"Tell me everything you know," she ordered.

"If I did that," he said with a wry twist of the lips, "you'd never believe me."

"I'll do my best to keep an open mind."

His smile faded as he turned to look over the cove. "Unfortunately, I learned nothing new about what happened to the Destan ship."

When she opened her mouth to protest, he lifted a hand to silence her.

"That *is* the truth, Princess Reva, I swear on my life. I'm still uneasy though. You should be extra careful until we figure out what's going on." He hesitated, his hand straying to the pocket that held Calix. "Whatever happened yesterday…I don't think it was from natural causes."

"What do you mean?"

"I mean," he answered, stressing the words, "that I think magic was involved."

An itch rose on the back of Reva's neck and shivered down her spine. First Rency talking about curses, and now Jareth and magic… *What* had *happened to the Endellion?*

CHAPTER SIX

Before Reva had a chance to answer, someone shouted her name.

She spun, her fingers itching to reach for the dagger in her boot, but it was only Cassandra who had finished her morning toilette surprisingly early. Her stepmother waved for Reva to join her at the fire.

"We'll finish this discussion later," she whispered to Jareth.

Angry voices washed over her as she drew closer. She could smell the flattened rice cakes the *Perseus's* cook was preparing for breakfast, a common morning dish topped with cardamom. Isla and the cook both crouched beside the fire, and Reva would have given her own left leg to join them. Her stomach growled, but breakfast wouldn't be headed her way anytime soon.

Not if the bickering had already commenced.

Nothing to be done for it, she told herself staunchly. *Might as well have the meeting.* With any luck, she'd be able to enjoy her breakfast afterwards, in peace and quiet.

"It's rude to make Prince Felix wait," Cassandra said, smoothing the folds of her green silk dress as Reva approached with Jareth at her heels. She raked her gaze over Reva's appearance and pursed her lips. Isla rose and turned from the fire, holding a steaming pewter mug in her hands. She made a face behind Cassandra's back, then circled the regent to hand Reva the mug.

"Wait for what?" Reva asked, accepting the cup of steaming coffee and carefully avoiding eye contact with the first mate, lest she be tempted to laugh at the sailor's antics. "Are we resuming discussions before breakfast?"

Cassandra's narrowed eyes rimmed with dark kohl. She looked worthy of a court appearance and was far too overdressed for negotiations on a barren rock island.

"We haven't discussed yet how I'm going to get home," Felix said, his sunburned cheeks even redder than usual. "I want to go home right away."

"Felix," Cassandra said, her voice soothing and playful, "why are you in such a hurry? If you wait a day or two, you can take Reva with you—"

"I don't want to wait."

"Felix, if this is what's worrying you, please put it from your mind." Reva nearly rolled her eyes but held herself still. "Rest assured, someone will make sure you get home."

What a self-centered prick.

"Either that, or we'll leave you here with plenty of food and supplies and send word to your people to dispatch ships for you. That is, if you don't trust my crew to see to your wellbeing…"

"No, no, that's unacceptable!" Fury and something akin to panic twisted his face. "I demand you and your mother—"

"Stepmother," Reva interrupted, earning a glare from Lady Cassandra.

"—take me home *at once*," he blustered. "That is the only acceptable solution for a prince!"

"A third prince, and not at all likely to gain the throne."

Reva jumped at the whisper in her ear. Rency had oozed his way in between her and Jareth, just like Calix worming his way around her tent and pocket, trying to make himself at home someplace where he didn't belong.

She patted her pocket just to make sure it was still empty. It was, thank the sands.

"Does that matter?" she whispered, frowning at Rency. "As a royal, he is within his rights to request transport."

Although…perhaps transportation was something she could use to her advantage in the negotiations?

"Request, yes. Demand, no," Rency said into her ear. "If I were you, I'd be leery of him. Felix isn't to be trusted."

He needn't have worried, because she had no intentions of trusting the Deotan prince after he'd teamed up with Cassandra behind her back, but she wondered if Rency knew anything she didn't. What had he really wanted to talk to her about last night?

"I'll not be dismissed!" Felix stabbed his pointer finger toward the ground, trying to make some sort of point. "My concerns will not be dismissed!"

Cassandra patted his arm. "Felix, my boy, no one is trying to dismiss your concerns."

Unfortunately, even Cassandra's charms could only go so far.

"No, no!" Felix slashed his palm through the air. "Not only am I down a ship and a third of my crew, but I've been robbed, as well!"

"Robbed?" Rency asked with sudden curiosity.

Reva could have sworn she caught a gleam of humor in his eye. Or was it only interest in the unfolding drama? What had he pilfered from Felix?

"Yes, robbed!"

Her missing earrings suddenly floated to the forefront of her thoughts. "What's been stolen?" Reva tried to ask.

However, as before, her question was superseded by the prince's loud declaration: "I think we all know who's responsible!"

Is this what a marriage to him would be like? Him always talking over me? His voice lifted over mine? Suppressing mine?

Reva scarcely had time to acknowledge the thought, to tuck it away as a real concern, before Prince Felix was pointing at *her*. She frowned, her head rearing back in affront. Then she realized he was pointing at someone behind her.

Jareth moved to stand beside her, crossing his arms over his chest. The tiniest pink tentacle draped itself over the edge of one of his pockets.

Not the pocket he'd dropped Calix into either.

So Jareth definitely had more than one of his little friends on him.

"You think the sea elves robbed you?" Reva asked with practiced calm. "Really, Felix, what did you bring on this trip that was so important it was worth stealing?"

"I'm merely stating the obvious—that a great many strange occurrences have happened since this...*person*...arrived."

Although he said *person*, Felix's tone implied Jareth was something far less than that. Indignation on Jareth's behalf ignited inside Reva, simmering beneath the placid expression she pasted on her face.

"On my life, I have stolen nothing from you" Jareth said, voice stilted. "I'm innocent of these charges."

"Oh, you're innocent. How lovely for me." Felix snorted. "My signet ring is still gone."

"Not by my hand," Jareth said in a low, tight voice, but he shifted his stance and swept a hand down his side.

The kraken arm disappeared in a flash.

Felix narrowed his gaze and then jabbed a finger toward Rency. "Him, then! He took it!"

"Oy, that's jolly unfair!" Rency lifted both hands defensively. "I'm not a petty criminal."

Isla choked and coughed violently.

Reva lifted her mug and finally allowed herself a sip. The hot, bitter liquid filled her mouth and warmed her from the inside out as it slid down her throat. Taking a deep breath, she cleared her throat. "We can continue to accuse one another with no proof to support our accusations," she said, pausing to take another sip of coffee, "or we can eat breakfast and continue with our negotiations. I cannot speak for the rest of you, but I'm hungry."

Distrusting glances were exchanged by nearly all parties before Isla clapped her hands and shattered the silence. "What a fine idea! Everyone thinks better with food in their bellies. Heave, ho, maties! Fill your bellies with these *delicious* rice cakes, made by the hand of the most famous chef on the high seas."

She waved a hand toward the *Perseus*'s cook, who flushed as red as Felix's sunburn and held out a platter of rice cakes.

"Oh, be quiet," Cassandra growled as she shoved past Isla, snatched a rice cake off the platter, and stormed toward the awning higher up the beach.

Reva grinned at the first mate as she selected her warm rice cake from the cook's platter. She graced him with a smile as well. "They are the best on the seas," she whispered with a wink.

The cook's embarrassed smile widened.

Breakfast was only a slight delay of the inevitable bickering.

For her part, Reva might have happily burrowed her head in the sand or thrown her arms over her head to block out her stepmother insisting that, of course Reva would honor the agreement and marry Prince Felix.

Or Felix blustering that he'd not journeyed all this way to go home with less than he'd arrived with.

Or Rency declaring he would only accept a despicable amount of coin for safe passage through his territory…or the hand of a princess. Either was fine by him but preferably both.

Prince Jareth remained quiet throughout the discussions, speaking only when pressed but always watching and listening.

Reva just wanted the endless arguing to stop.

She lifted pained eyes when Isla approached, stooping to whisper in her ear. "You look like you're in need of rescue. Consider this your invitation to step away and deal with some vital matter regarding the ship."

Reva suppressed a grin.

"Excuse me, gentlemen, stepmother," she said as she launched to her feet and brushed off the back of her skirt. "It appears there is an important matter I must attend to."

Before anyone could try to stop her, Reva allowed Isla to whisk her from beneath the awning, reveling in the few precious moments to herself.

Isla released a long sigh. "I don't envy you, Princess," she said, her steady footsteps causing the sand to squeak beneath her boots. "I suppose some might look at your life and call it glamorous, but I look at what you're enduring and realize how grateful I am to find my livelihood at sea."

"Don't try to make me jealous." Reva shook her head. "I don't know what to do, Isla. I fear my wisest course truly is to marry Felix. *Felix!*"

"You can't do that!" The masculine whisper hissed from behind caused both girls to spin around.

Rency dogged their footsteps, his hair billowing in the wind.

Reva's temper finally fizzled over. "If you know what's good for you, you'll go back to the group. I don't want to deal with you right now, Rency. Five minutes of peace. Can't I ask for that much?"

"Um…no. I don't think you can." The fellow laughed, giving his head a shake to toss his dark—blonde hair out of his eyes. "I was only on my way to the shore. A longboat has arrived from the *Andromeda*. I'm going to see why."

"Uh huh." Isla sounded entirely unconvinced.

"Off you go, then," Reva said between her teeth. She wiggled her fingers in a shooing motion.

He flashed her a grin, then sobered. "Back to Felix, love. I truly believe you should weigh the matter carefully." To Rency's credit, all traces of the devil-may-care fellow were gone—even his charming dimple had vanished. Sincerity blanketed his tone and his features. "I wouldn't trust Felix with a leaky boat, let alone something as important as my future."

"What do you know, Rency?"

The captain pursed his lips and glanced over his shoulder before leaning toward Reva. "I heard he's fallen out of favor with his father," he said in a low tone. "And a man out of favor is desperate, and desperate men are dangerous."

Reva absorbed the information in silence. If Felix had lost the backing of his father…could he even *offer* trade routes? Or was something else going on here?

He pressed a hand to her arm, held her gaze a fraction too long, and then swept across the beach, the wind whipping the billowing sleeves of his barely laced tunic.

Isla whistled. "I may not like that wretched fool, but you have to admit he's handsome. You sure you don't want to consider *his* proposal?"

"Absolutely not." Reva raked her best friend with a withering look.

"Hm, well, I might take him then. Just to mend his poor bleeding heart after you break it." Isla cast a wistful look over her shoulder at the pirate captain's retreating form, then spun about to keep pace with Reva. "Although, I confess I would prefer you consider the pirate over the prince. Felix is…" Isla didn't finish the thought.

Reva cast a glance toward the awning and the group still gathered there. Felix's loud, blustery tones rose above the rest.

"But we need trade routes, and if the way to get them is marriage to Felix…" She let her words fade into stilted silence.

Isla placed a hand on Reva's elbow and squeezed. "I don't like the sum of your figures, dearie."

The truly disheartening thing about the whole matter was that Reva didn't disagree with Isla or Rency about Felix's lack of good qualities, but what if marrying the prince of Desta was the *only* way to ensure her people didn't starve? Did she not owe it to her people to do what was necessary, even if it made her sick inside? A desperate part of her feared she had no choice. Fate had already made the decision for her.

She had no choice but to lay everything at the feet of a man who would grind her hopes, dreams, and sacrifices beneath his boots without a second thought.

After an agonizing day of negotiations that led nowhere, the dilemma plagued Reva long into the night. Again, she could not sleep, her heart sore over the threat to Etthan's future…to her future. She heaved a sigh and rolled onto her side.

Footsteps squeaked against the sand outside her tent. Reva's heart jumped into her throat as she grabbed for the dagger at her side. Although the person was clearly making no effort to hide their approach, Reva went cold with dread.

"Oy, Highness? You awake?" Isla's familiar voice instantly soothed Reva's fears.

"Isla. Shouldn't you be on board ship?" she whispered, leaving her mattress to push aside the tent flap to address her friend.

The first mate held a storm lantern, its light covered except for the tiny pinpricks of holes. Isla ducked to enter the tent, her eyes ringed with dark circles. "After what happened last night, I decided to spend the night here," she said, also keeping her voice low. "But I think something's wrong."

Reva shoved her tangled hair out of her eyes and reached for her boots. "What do you mean, something's wrong?"

"Albus? He just arrived in the rowboat with a message. He said everyone on board is asleep."

"Asleep?" Reva yanked her boots on, one after the other, and then slid her dagger into the hidden sheath. "I don't understand—"

"*Everyone's* asleep," Isla cut her short. "Even the watchmen. Poor Albus said it felt like a ghost ship. Captain Dren and I were most vigilant to set guards…so why is everyone on that blasted ship asleep except the powder monkey?"

"Where is Captain Dren?" Reva asked.

She felt around in the dim lighting for her long coat. Despite the warmer temperatures of the day, breezes off the sea cooled down the island at night, and it was chilly.

"He's supposed to be aboard ship," Isla said. Reva noted the fear in her tones. "That concerns me. He's far too good a captain to allow the crew to slack at their duties."

"I don't like this." Reva slipped into her coat. "Do you think they were drugged? Enchanted?"

"I haven't a clue." Isla backed out of the tent and Reva followed. The island slept around them, deathly quiet. A fire burned at the center of the rock, close to the awning. The watchmen stood in alert poses, looking right at Reva and Isla. Reva glanced that way as she and the first mate headed to the sea, considering calling out to them.

No. They had a job to do here.

She should not draw them away from Cassandra. In any event, she didn't know for sure that anything was wrong. Albus could be mistaken. He was young. Maybe he was making more of this than he should.

At the water's edge, they met Albus. His own storm lantern sat in the boat, the pricks of light drawing Reva's gaze to the boy's heavy overcoat and nervous pacing.

"Are you ready, first mate?" he asked, teeth chattering. He avoided looking Reva in the eye.

"Ready," Isla said. "Let's cast off."

Reva frowned. Albus wasn't usually so shy around her, and it wasn't *that* cold. She felt a knot forming in the pit of her stomach. Something wasn't right, but she couldn't quite put her finger on what.

If he came all the way here alone to tell us what's happening aboard the ship, no wonder he's nervous.

Reva helped shove the boat into the water, ignoring the water sloshing against her boots, then hopped into the rowboat. Along with Isla, she grabbed an oar and commenced rowing. As they moved over the choppy waves, Reva wondered if Jareth was down there somewhere…watching them.

It always made her a little nervous how dark and deep the ocean felt at night. Although the ships were anchored just offshore, the lanterns offered only minute illumination. *It would be easy to be lost at sea during the night,* she mused as she rowed. But she had full faith in Isla and Albus's ability to get them safely to the *Perseus*.

Soon enough, they bumped up against the hull. "I'll hold the ladder," Albus said. "Climb aboard."

Isla went first. Grabbing onto the rope ladder, Reva steadied herself. She watched her friend's ankles disappearing into the gloom. Sucking in a breath, Reva attempted to calm the nerves in her stomach. Although she'd made the climb onto the deck of a ship many times, she'd never done it when it was black as tar outside.

You'll be fine, she told herself once more and hoisted her body onto the ladder.

Isla certainly managed the climb with more speed than her. In fact, oddly, by the time Reva got close to the railing, she heard voices and murmurs. A frown pinched between her brows. Hadn't Albus claimed everyone on board was asleep?

He must have been mistaken about everyone being asleep, which meant this had all been a false alarm.

Was it, though? As she reached out and grabbed the wooden railing, she heard Isla's voice, "Get your—"

But the words broke off abruptly.

Reva faltered. Who on the *Perseus* would have the nerve to silence Isla, the first mate and favored of the princess?

"Isla?" she called to the darkness above her.

There was no response.

Dread pooling in her stomach, Reva wondered if she could grip her dagger in one hand and still climb. She opted to slip the blade between her teeth. Then she had to decide if she would continue boarding her ship. But it was either climb on deck or go back down the ladder, and she could hear Albus scrambling up from below, blocking a descent.

And if she didn't behave as expected, what would happen to Isla?

So, Reva ground her teeth together and finished the climb, leveraging her body over the railing and dropping lightly onto the deck.

Thump.

Before she had a chance to grab the dagger from between her teeth, hands grabbed her from both sides. She shrieked around the dagger in her mouth and felt fingers probing her face.

"The bonny lass has a blade between her teeth," someone whispered, half laughing. "You know how to pick 'em, Cap."

Cap? As in…

"Keep a civil tongue in your mouth, mate," said a certain silky-voiced pirate.

CHAPTER SEVEN

Heat washed over Reva in uncomfortable waves. What the devil? Why was Rency on board the *Perseus?*

Rency appeared out of the shadows, his angular face illuminated by the storm lanterns hanging nearby. He leaned over Reva and grabbed the handle of her dagger. She ground her teeth together as hard as she could and shrieked at him, yanking furiously at the hands holding her arms behind her back.

"Don't be like that, love," Rency whispered as he jiggled the dagger, jarring her teeth up and down as he attempted to extract her one and only weapon. He seemed loath to simply yank it out—which would surely slice her lips open.

Apparently, he wanted her alive and unspoiled.

Reva struck out with one foot, but he knocked her boot to the side with a gentle kick of his own.

"You promised they'd not be harmed." Albus spoke over her captors' scuffle, his voice trembling.

"And they won't be," Rency said, still wiggling the dagger between Reva's teeth. "Good man for bringing her to us. You'll be handsomely rewarded just as we discussed."

Rency had paid that baby-faced cabin boy to betray her?

Reva screamed between her teeth just as Rency succeeded in stealing her blade. It scraped against the tips of her teeth, creating a bone-chilling sound in her head. She winced and spat at the pirate captain in a most un-princess-like manner.

He just laughed.

Fury and frustration tore through her, and she stomped madly for the toes of the men who imprisoned her, but they shoved her to her knees. She felt the point of a sword at the back of her neck.

"Don't fight it, Princess," someone said in her ear. "You'll just make this more difficult."

Reva froze, chest heaving with angry breaths. "Where's my first mate?"

After a momentary pause, Isla swore. "I'm here, Highness." She sounded furious. "Oy, put that foul hand over my mouth again, and you'll be carrying my teeth around as trophies for the rest of your sorry life."

A snicker echoed around the group of pirates.

Rency flicked a look toward Isla, the corner of his mouth curving upward in another of his infuriating smiles.

"Rency promised you'd not be hurt." Albus tried to defend himself.

"I'll keelhaul you!" Isla snarled. "See if I don't have your hide stretched out to tan in the sun when I get my hands on you."

Before Albus could answer, Rency called quietly over his shoulder, "Cast off, boys!"

"Wait!" Reva tried to push herself upright, but the sword at her neck nipped harder against her skin, halting her. "Rency, where are we going? What are you doing? I took you for a blackguard, but I never took you for a kidnapper and hijacker! The *Perseus* is my flagship, and you've no—"

"I'm no mere kidnapper." Rency squatted in front of her, so close she could see the lantern light flickering in his eyes. "I'm saving your life, love. You should reward me with a kiss."

"I'll reward you all right," she said, lacing her words with venom. "You can kiss your treasure goodbye, along with any chance you ever had of becoming a reputable merchant. You've sealed your fate, pirate."

He sighed and plastered a wounded look on his lying face. "Alas, you're probably right. I never was one to play by the rules. But I'm not a hijacker. You aren't on the *Perseus,* poppet."

Reva's breath hitched, and she craned her head to look around. The lanterns lit so little of the deck that it took her a moment to accept the truth of his words. This wasn't the *Perseus.*

"Aye, this is the *Andromeda.* I'm no ship thief: this is *my* flagship."

Her heart rate stuttered, then escalated again. "That doesn't matter. Your actions are still a blatant act of war—"

"Oh, let the poor dithering maiden up." Rency ran a hand over his face as if she plagued him nye to death. "Let them both up."

As the sword withdrew from her nape, Reva bounded to her feet, her hands balled into fists. She'd show him just how much of a *dithering maiden* she was. "I trusted you, Rency," she snarled. "I gave you a chance when no one else would."

The truth slammed into her like a fist, his betrayal worming deep into her heart. She'd trusted him, her *one* ally in this horrible nightmare. And now this…

"Now, now, Reva." Rency raised his hands placatingly. "I swear on my honor, I don't intend you any harm. In fact, I brought you on board my ship for your own safety. To protect you from Felix."

"To protect me from—" She couldn't believe what she was hearing. "*You* are the one who's hauled me off into the night. You're protecting me by *kidnapping me?*"

"I told you he was not to be trusted," Rency countered. "You weren't listening, Reva, darling. Rather, you seemed to be leaning toward accepting his ridiculous marriage proposal." He shuddered as if something with gooey tentacles had crawled over the back of his neck.

"What business is it of yours? Sand and pearls, I was never going to marry *you*! So why would you care?"

"I care because we're *friends,* and that's what friends do—"

"Oy, Cap!" Footsteps thundered toward them, half a dozen of Rency's crew scuffling out of the darkness with something in front of them.

Someone.

Prince Jareth's knees hit the deck with a jarring thud, and he glared up at Rency, his sea green eyes glinting with anger. He snarled something around the gag in his mouth and yanked furiously against the sailors pinning his arms behind his back.

"By the fates, what is *he* doing here?" Rency asked, flapping a hand toward the hog-tied elvish prince. "I didn't place an order for any princes, you worthless dogs. I wanted a princess. One. Her. Not him. Where'd you get him, anyway?"

"From the sea," one of the sailors admitted. "We hauled him up in a net like a fish."

"Well, toss him back in like a fish then. I don't have any use for him, and I don't want to start a war with the ocean, you fools."

"But he was snooping around, Cap," the smallest of the sailors whined. "We didn't want him swimming back to the beach and spinning tales."

Rency shrugged. "By the time he gets to shore, we'll have a decent head start. Enough of a lead to make this fun."

"What will be fun is hanging you from the yardarm and watching you twitch in the breeze," Reva said, filling her words with anger to hide the pain that burned beneath the surface. "Whatever you're trying to do here, Rency, kidnapping *two* royals and starting a war with not one but *three* kingdoms is not going to be good for your health."

Rency held her gaze, his cocky smile growing wider by the second. "Ah, but when have I ever cared about my health, darling girl?"

The sea prince wrenched against his captors again, mumbling around the gag in his mouth. The sailors struggled to hold him down.

"What's that? I can't understand you," Rency said, his tone and smile so amiable it made Reva want to punch him in the face. Repeatedly.

"Rency, take that gag out his mouth at once," Reva barked.

The pirate captain shrugged and snapped his fingers. "If you wish to listen to him bellow and whine, be my guest. This is getting tiresome, though. I need a nap."

"You need a spanking," Reva said as she strode forward and knelt in front of Prince Jareth.

She worked her fingers around the knotted kerchief the pirates had used to gag him. Jareth stared at her hard, an indiscernible glint in his eyes. She slowed her movements and held his gaze. What was he thinking?

When the gag slid free, Jareth worked his jaw side to side and licked his lips. "Thank you, Your Highness," he said. "That rag tasted incredibly foul."

One of the sailors snickered, but he choked into silence when Reva shot him a withering glare.

"Now," Reva said, still kneeling in front of Jareth. "What did you wish to say, Your Highness?"

"I wanted to say that I don't think Felix is the one we need to worry about." Jareth leaned a fraction closer to her.

"Of course he is!" Rency threw his arms wide, as if he were an actor on a stage making some sort of grand gesture. "He's a nincompoop."

"I've been watching the cove," Jareth said, focusing on Reva. "There's something in the water."

Something? Why was he being so vague? Unless…unless he didn't *know* what was in the cove? What sort of creature would be a mystery to a prince of the sea?

"Of course there are things in the water. It's an *ocean*," Rency said with a wounded sniff. "But I agree. We've sat here long enough. Why isn't this bucket of boards and rusty nails moving?" He stomped his foot against the deck like a petulant child. A sound echoed from the bowels of the ship that could only be described as a belch.

Reva's eyebrows lifted.

"None of that," Rency snarled, stomping his boot yet again. "Move! Or I'll take you apart, one board at a time and sell you for kindling!"

The *Andromeda* lurched, rocking Reva forward. Gasping, she caught herself, bracing one hand against the vibrating deck of the ship and the other against Jareth's arm. Her fingers curled around firm muscle. The sailor's holding Jareth in place regained their footing then tightened their grips on his arms.

"Easy," Jareth whispered. "We'll get out of this, Princess." He'd spoken the words impossibly low, for her ears alone.

She let her hand linger on his arm as she searched his eyes for some sign of deceit—she wasn't feeling terribly trusting at the moment—but she couldn't guess what he was thinking. With a frustrated exhale, she let her fingers slide from his arm and rose, turning to face their kidnapper.

"Can you at least release Prince Jareth and Isla? We're not foolish enough to dive overboard in the middle of the cove."

Rency ran his fingers over the railing of the ship and gave it a pat before looking up to acknowledge Reva. "You're too clever, yes, but that one—" He pointed to Jareth. "—is a fish out of water. And while I am loath to admit that these idiots of mine possess even an ounce of common sense…I would rather not sound the alarm until we're further out to sea."

Reva flexed her fingers and curled them into fists. The motion sent prickles of pain through the cut on her arm. "Take care, Rency," she said in a voice as cold as the sea itself. "I'll not stand for my citizens being clapped in irons in the belly of your blasted ship."

"And what do you intend to do to stop me?" He lifted her dagger and used the tip of the blade *to pick his rotten teeth*.

Her mouth worked soundlessly. She'd never be able to use her weapon again.

Clenching her fists tighter, she darted to the left, ducked around the snatching arm of a pirate, and leaped neatly onto the railing Rency had been stroking only moments before. Arms held out to the side to maintain her balance, she stared out into the darkness of the night.

"I'll jump," she warned, praying to every star in the night sky that she wouldn't get dizzy and actually tumble headfirst into the pitch—black water. "Unless you release Isla and Prince Jareth, I'll jump."

Silence coiled around her as the *Andromeda* continued to forge a path away from Black Rock. Then Rency cursed.

"You are the most annoying princess I have ever met. Why can't you be one of those useless, frilly sorts who vomit at the sight of a ship?"

"If you wanted a vomiting royal, you should have kidnapped Felix."

"Clearly."

Reva's legs began to tremble from the strain, her lower back aching from the awkwardness of her position. "Do we have a deal, Rency?"

A swell knocked against the *Andromeda,* and she battled to maintain her precarious balance.

"Aye, aye! We have a deal!" he shouted close behind her. "Get your skinny arse off that railing *now*!"

"Release them first."

"Reva—"

Another shudder shook the boat. Reva's feet slipped, and she only had enough time to gasp before she plummeted. Her head smacked against unyielding wood, and the blackness of oblivion ripped her away.

Reva woke to drowning.

Salt water flooded her throat, suffocating her, and she thrashed as panic overran her befuddled mind. Her entire world became nothing but fear and pain.

Nothing but cold and endless darkness.

Then arms wrapped around her waist, and she was moving upward through bone—cold water. Her head broke the surface, but a swell immediately sucked her back into the sea. The arm around her waist clung more tightly. She broke to the surface again and fought to make her lungs work.

Air. She needed air.

Now!

But the absence of air was all she knew, a void so expansive everything else shrank to a pinprick and vanished.

The faintest notes of music teased her ears as she soundlessly worked her mouth, trying to find the breaths that eluded her. Was it the song of the afterlife calling her name?

Her chest burned as the discordant notes coalesced into a song as beautiful and deadly as the sea fighting to claim her soul for its own.

She sank beneath the waves once more.

Hands cupped her face on either side, and something pressed against her face, sealing her mouth. She jerked, the last shreds of her strength battling against the ocean creature trying to smother her.

The music grew louder and louder, terrible and enthralling—a killing song, a melody that could break hearts or topple kingdoms.

The thing pressed against her face moved gently, sending a flood of warmth into her lips, her mouth, her throat…

Her lungs tightened and expanded.

Relief exploded into every corner of her body. Life trickled through her veins as the air she so desperately needed somehow filled her lungs. How was she alive? She wasn't breathing, her body still floating beneath angry waves, her limbs tangled with those of another. And yet she *was* breathing.

She suddenly became very aware of the arm around her waist, of the chest breathing with her—no, breathing *for* her.

Together, they moved with the sounds of the sea, rising and sinking with the music of the ocean. What sort of devilry was this?

What sort of…sea magic?

Jareth?

A thumb brushed against her jaw, the rest of his fingers tangled in her hair, clasping the back of her head to keep her close. His mouth moved against hers, gentle but persistent as the magic of his kiss kept her alive.

A siren kiss.

Horror mingled with wonder. She'd thought siren kisses spelled doom for sailors. And yet…she wasn't dying. Life hummed through her veins, so strong she wondered if she'd ever truly *known* life before this moment. How was this possible?

Reva clutched the front of Jareth's tunic, silently begging him not to let go, not to release her into this dark and terrible sea to die alone.

Not now when she felt so alive.

She shifted her arm to wrap it around his neck, imprisoning him in her hold. She was *never* letting go.

CHAPTER EIGHT

Rough hands jerked Reva from the icy water, yanking her out of Jareth's warm, protective arms. Her teeth chattered as she slumped unceremoniously onto the seat in a dinghy. She huddled over her knees, trying to preserve the last trickles of warmth in her core as it leaked out of her.

Her head *hurt*.

The dinghy rocked precariously, and Jareth dropped onto the seat beside her. She didn't try to look at him as he draped an arm across her back. She wasn't sure she wanted to look at him, to face what had happened between them underwater.

"Give her some space, man," Rency said from behind them in the dinghy.

"No!" Jareth's sharp voice echoed across the waters. "She needs to touch me. Get your hands off me unless you want to take another swim."

Reva tried to grind her teeth together to keep them from chattering but gave up. Jareth brushed her soaking hair from her face and pressed his palm over her forehead.

Warmth spread from her head, over her cheekbones, down over her lips and quivering jaw. The dinghy rocked as the sailors across from them rowed.

She twisted to look Jareth in the face. "T-that h-h-helps," she said.

He smiled grimly and moved his hand to press against the back of her neck. Again, a delicious flood of warmth leaked from his palm into her chilled body. Even the throbbing pain in the back of her skull eased.

Jareth moved to grab her hands next, cupping them between his own as her shivering finally began to abate. She peeked at him from beneath her lashes. She could almost feel his mouth against hers again, a memory that clung to her skin in a physical way… Did he often use his siren kiss on drowning maidens? Was it possible that kiss— or whatever it was—meant something to him?

Or was he just saving her life?

She averted her gaze, not sure she wanted to know the answers to her own questions. A different kind of heat warmed her cheeks. She'd never kissed anyone like *that* before.

Of course, she'd never been drowning before either. If she had to die, it would have been nice to go out with a kiss.

"Now how'd you do that, mate?" Rency's voice shattered the moment. He leaned down between them from where he had been standing in the prow of the boat, out of her line of sight.

Reva turned, ready to rip into him but hesitated when she saw the water glistening on his cheeks. Rency's blond locks were plastered against his head, and he seemed to be shuddering nearly as badly as she had been.

Had he jumped into the ocean after her as well?

"Don't suppose you'd share some of that heat magic, would you?" Rency asked, shivering. "I'm cold too."

"No," Jareth bit out without hesitation.

Reva smirked at Rency and allowed herself the pleasure of feeling—and looking—smug.

"Oh." Disappointment colored the pirate captain's tone, and he eased backward a few inches. But then he was between them again, so close Reva could have counted the water droplets running down his sun-browned skin. "Well, at least tell me how you did it then. You two were under water for nearly ten minutes. How'd you keep her alive?"

Reva's mind screeched to a blinding halt.

Ten minutes?

Jareth said nothing as he ran his hands down her arms. Steam began to rise from the fabric of her sleeves. She could feel the water dissipating, replaced by warm, drying fabric.

"Come on. How'd you do it?"

Still Jareth said nothing. Reva, more curious than Rency—if that were possible—also tried to catch the sea elf's eye, but he avoided looking at either of them.

Then Rency groaned. "Oh…oh, you didn't. By the bones of my ancestors…you used the siren kiss on her, didn't you?"

A muscle twitched in Jareth's cheek. He looked at Reva but dropped his gaze nearly as quickly when he caught her watching him.

"That's blasted unfair, mate. The rest of us don't stand a chance if you go around enchanting fair princesses with your sneaky ocean magic."

While Reva couldn't argue that enchantment had been involved, she was surprised Rency cared more about kissing than drowning. "S-s-song magic," she said. "I heard a s-s-song."

She looked to Jareth for answers, but his angular face with its high cheekbones, taut mouth, and deep-set eyes revealed nothing. In the dark, his eyes looked more like deep water—fathomless and dark—rather than the aquamarine of the shallows.

Rency dove between them again, squinting into her face. "Did you say *song magic*? He used the Sea Song on you too? The gig is up now, Reva. What a mess!" He groaned dramatically and retreated once again. "Our love story ended far too quickly—cut short by elvish trickery."

What's a Sea Song?

"Our love s-s-story never started." She tossed the words over her shoulder. "You n-n-never stood a chance, Rency. Especially after tonight."

Rency's eyes narrowed, but a smile played about his lips. "You're still planning to hang me then? Really, Reva. I thought better of you."

"T-t-take me back to Black Rock, Rency."

"No." Rency spit over the side of the dinghy and settled back against the seat with his arms folded over his chest.

He was still smiling.

Jareth's arm settled around Reva's shoulders again and tightened. What was he thinking? She couldn't see his face without repositioning and making it obvious she wanted to look at him. The dinghy bumped against the hull of the *Andromeda*. Waves sloshed over the side of the craft and nearly drowned Reva yet again.

"Hello, Beautiful." Rency cheerfully patted the hull of the ship, which creaked in response to his greeting.

A ladder dropped over the side, and Rency skittered up and out of sight without a backward glance at the rest of them. Jareth caught her elbow and helped her stand and turn to face the front of the dinghy. Her legs shook as she stepped over the bench and reached for the rungs of the ladder. She paused to catch her breath.

"I can carry you up." Jareth's voice brought a flush of heat to her cheeks, and she became more aware of the fingers still gripping her wrist. His fingers brushed the edge of the makeshift bandage Rency had wrapped around her arm.

Embarrassment and something else she wasn't ready to name sliced through her.

"I can manage on my own," she said, more curtly than she'd intended.

Jareth's hand fell away, and she placed her foot on the bottom rung. However, by the time she reached the top, she almost wished she'd taken him up on the gallant offer. She could barely move as Rency and one of his sailors pulled her over the railing and set her feet on the creaking deck. Rency pulled her away from the railing and shoved her down on a barrel.

"No more falling overboard for you," he said, patting her on the head before he returned to the railing to make sure Jareth and the other two sailors boarded without incident.

Someone yelped behind Reva. She turned to watch as Isla darted away from a sailor bent over, hugging his stomach and groaning in pain. Isla threw her arms around Reva and held her tightly. "You stupid, stupid girl," she said in Reva's ear as she eased back and brushed Reva's hair out of her face.

Reva blinked at her, shivering hard without Jareth to keep her warm. "S-s-sorry for trying to save your life."

"It isn't your job to protect me." Isla slapped Reva's cheek gently, something no one else on the seas would ever dare to do. "Never put yourself in danger like that again. Not for me. Understand?"

Reva nodded, although she really didn't have any intention of obeying.

As soon as Jareth's bare feet hit the deck, he also stepped toward Reva, but Rency snapped his fingers to summon two sailors. They grabbed Jareth by the arms and halted him halfway to Reva.

"Find him a bunk," Rency said without emotion. He flicked a hand toward Isla. "And take that one too."

Jareth struggled as they shoved him down the gangway to the lower levels of the ship.

When a sailor reached for Reva's arm, Isla swung a fist toward his face. He dodged back with a yelp, and Rency shouted an impatient, "Not the princess, you lout. Take the other one."

"The one trying to break my nose?" The pirate caught Isla's fist and shoved it away.

"Aye, that one. Lock her up with the elf."

Reva tried to stand on wobbling legs. "No, I want Isla to stay with me—"

But no one listened. Her voice had no authority here.

Three sailors converged on Isla, catching her by the arm and tunic as they dragged her away from Reva. Reva stumbled after them, but her legs weren't working right, and she went down on one knee. Isla curled her legs to her chest as kicked out as the pirates hauled her toward the hold. A fourth sailor caught her ankles. Reva shouted angrily as they practically threw the first mate down the narrow stairs leading below deck.

Rising again, Reva staggered toward Rency on weak legs, not sure what she intended to do, but it wasn't going to be nice.

He merely stepped to the side and swept a gallant hand—not toward the hold—but toward the quarterdeck. When she skidded to a halt and shook her head defiantly, he snapped his fingers and marched off without her. A burly sailor muttered an apology as he caught her by the elbows and shoved her across the deck in Rency's wake. The heels of her soaked boots skidded uselessly across the planks.

When the sailor tried to push her into the captain's cabin, Reva grabbed the doorframe. Rency laughed from inside. "Stop being such a pain, Reva."

The sailor jostled her inside and shoved her into a chair at a small table strewn with maps, parchment, books, compass, spyglass, and various other instruments. Rency retreated across the cabin, head and shoulders half submerged in a massive trunk. He tossed various items onto the floor before he finally pulled out a thick wad of fabric. Striding toward Reva, he held it out to her.

She took it without thinking and raked him with a frown as her fingers sank into silky folds. The rose—hued item dropped onto her lap, overflowing with lace, ribbons, and far too much skirt.

"I'm not wearing this." She shoved the dress off her lap and let it plop to the floor beside her chair.

"You can't stay in your clothes," Rency said as he repacked the trunk and slammed the lid closed. "You'll catch your death in those wet things. Be a good girl, put on your dress, and climb into bed. No more fussing now."

Reva's gaze shot across the room to the spacious bunk along the far wall. Panic flooded her veins again. "Oh, no. Absolutely not! I am *not*—"

"I won't be sleeping in the bed with you, Reva," Rency said as he stooped beside her chair to receive the dress. His voice and inflection lacked all its customary mirth as he shoved the dress into her arms again. "That bed is yours until you leave my ship. As is the cabin. Don't be a fool and make this harder. Just get dressed and go to bed. We'll talk in the morning…when you're in a better mood."

He left her sitting in the chair, arms full of enough dress to decently clothe three women.

"I'm not sleeping in your bed, Rency!" she hollered after him.

"Then sleep on the floor, woman!"

The ship shook around her as the door slammed closed behind him.

But by the time she shed her soaked clothes, spread them over the back of Rency's chair to dry, and wrestled into the ridiculous dress, Rency's bed became too tempting to resist. She shoved the extra chair under the door handle and crawled, shivering, into the bunk.

She'd fight for different accommodations tomorrow.

And get rid of the dress too…this thing had way too much fabric.

The next morning, Reva woke to the smell of coffee. She'd been dreaming about swimming in the ocean with Jareth…more specifically…kissing Jareth.

Heat warmed her cheeks as she shoved aside Rency's blankets and swung her legs over the side of the bunk, kicking her skirt out of the way to free her ankles. The chair no longer stood between her and the door. Somehow, they'd broken in while she was asleep, put the chair back at the table, and left a platter on top of Rency's clutter.

The knowledge that someone had been in here while she slept made her feel vulnerable…and a little violated too. Frowning, Reva searched the room for the captain, but she was alone. Bookshelves as cluttered as the central table lined the wall adjacent to the bunk, across from the trunk and an intricately carved wardrobe.

She padded across the cabin and studied the contents of the tray: a mug of steaming coffee and a plate of fruit, biscuits, and dried herring. She tossed a dried date into her mouth and chewed as she dragged the chair back to the door and wedged it in place. Apparently, it wouldn't keep Rency out, but it would give her advanced warning when he wanted to barge in on her.

The hem of Rency's ridiculous dress whispered against the floor as she returned to the table. It was too big for her, hanging around her hips and dragging around her feet. She skidded to a halt, however, when she reached the table.

The clothes she'd draped across the back of Rency's chair were gone.

Curse that man! She clenched her fists and resisted the urge to throw something at the wall. Rency's large, throne-like chair was the only one left at the table, so Reva dropped into it and arranged her dress the way Cassandra would have liked her to.

Maybe she could put her stepmother's ridiculous rules and habits to good use.

Rency had made a mistake when he'd taken her by force, threatening the fragile friendship they'd built. He may think he'd stolen a princess who needed saving, but he was wrong.

He'd caught himself a feral queen.

CHAPTER NINE

Reva sipped her coffee and filled her growling stomach as she waited for the pirate captain to return. He'd show up eventually…like a bad penny or a toothache. The fluttering lace around her elbow-length sleeves itched as she stretched across the table to grab an apple. Polishing it on her shoulder, she had to admit the dress didn't look as awful after a good night's sleep. It was definitely frilly and impractical, with the ribbons criss-crossing up the front of the bodice and spitting out bunches of lace just above her bosom. But the skirt wasn't as voluminous as she'd thought.

Juicy fruit exploded in her mouth as she took a vicious bite of her apple. A dinner knife glittered on the table beside her. How thoughtful of Rency to leave it for her. He'd probably done it on purpose just so he could laugh when she tried to stab him in the back.

She'd surprise him by putting it to good use in other ways.

After breakfast, she used the knife to hack the dress into a more comfortable bit of attire. All the scratchy lace went first, as did the sash trailing down the back of her dress. She used the sash pieces to cinch up the front of the skirt, stabbing holes in the waistline to secure the ties. While her clothes had disappeared, her boots and stockings still sat on the floor where she'd kicked them off.

When no one had appeared by the time she finished altering the dress, she decided she wouldn't wait for them to come for her. Returning the chair to its place at the table, Reva tested the door handle. It gave easily beneath her touch.

Interesting.

She took one last look around the room to see if she'd missed a better weapon than her table knife. Nothing of note stood out except for the large hat hanging beside the door with a ridiculously long feather sprouting from the brim. Reva snatched up the hat and plopped it on her hair, twirling the plume with her finger and hoping it would annoy Rency to have something of *his* pilfered without permission.

After taking a stabilizing breath, Reva flung open the door and stormed onto the deck of the *Andromeda* just in time to hear Isla bellow:

"You black-hearted pig! I challenge you to a duel!"

Isla stood in the center of the deck with a cutlass pointed at Rency's afore-mentioned black heart. The pirate captain stood motionless, focused on polishing his nails against his shirt rather than the woman threatening him with bodily harm. Reva wondered how Isla had even gotten her hands on a sword.

Reva eased onto the deck and inhaled a stabilizing breath as she tried to take stock of the situation. The sun beat down on the *Andromeda,* glistening off the white-capped waves beyond the deck railing. Pirates lounged around the deck, ignoring their duties. Even Jareth leaned against the main mast, arms folded as he watched the impending duel.

Was he hoping Isla would rid them of the pirate captain?

Rency glanced up from his nails and spotted Reva emerging from the cabin behind Isla. A smile split his face. "Reva, darling, you look marvelous—wait! Is that my hat?"

She twirled the plume again and raked him with a smile. "No. This is *my* hat," she said with icy coolness.

To Reva's left, Jareth coughed quietly, but she couldn't tell if he was masking amusement or approval.

"Fair enough," Rency conceded. "I did steal your clothes while you snored. You can keep the hat—" He broke off and his gaze drifted over the altered dress. Color drained from his face.

Reva twirled her plume again.

"What have you done to the dress?" He launched toward her but froze when Isla cut him off with a slash of her cutlass. Rency leaned to the left to see around Isla. "That dress belonged to my *mother!*"

Reva's determination to play the role of feral queen wilted beneath this revelation. "I assumed it belonged to someone in your harem."

"My—I don't have a *harem*. I don't have anyone, thanks to your elf prince and his magical lips."

At this, Jareth broke into a truly violent fit of coughing. Snickers rippled around the deck.

Rency ignored them all. "You should have asked before hacking my dress to pieces. What did you use anyway? Your teeth?"

The iron returned to her spine, and Reva forced away a stab of genuine remorse. "The table knife," she said. "It was nice of you to leave it for me."

"A mistake I won't repeat, let me tell you." Rency turned his back on her and braced his hands against the railing as he looked out over the endless sea.

Isla took advantage of the moment and smiled over her shoulder at Reva. "You look fabulous," she said.

Reva smiled in return before glancing toward Jareth, who had recovered from his embarrassment. Scarlet still stained his cheeks, however.

It was rather adorable, Reva decided.

Are you all right? his eyes seemed to ask.

She gave a curt nod to the unspoken question.

"Well, Rency," Isla goaded, twirling her cutlass, "am I going to get my duel, or no?"

"No," he said without turning away from the vista. "I don't duel with prisoners. I toss them overboard."

Isla barked a laugh. "Where's the fun in that, eh? What's the matter? You afraid of me?"

Rency only snorted.

"If that were true, you wouldn't have dove in after me last night," Reva countered.

At this, Rency finally spun to face her. Whatever hints of true emotion Reva thought she'd glimpsed moments before had vanished. A careless smile tore across his face. "What makes you think I jumped in after you?"

She pursed her lips briefly before matching his smile. "You were soaking wet, *love*," she said, letting the false endearment drip with sarcasm. "If you didn't jump in, then someone must have tossed *you* overboard. Or you fell. How embarrassing."

The crew guffawed loudly at this, but a growl from their captain sent them scuttling to their duties. They mopped and polished and checked the ropes without seeming to accomplish much.

Rency's cheek twitched. Then, abruptly, he bent at the waist and howled with laughter. The crew cast one another uncertain looks, but Rency waved a hand like a conductor leading a symphony. On cue, the sailors erupted into hoots and bellows, stomping their feet and pounding fists against railings. When Rency straightened and sliced a hand, they silenced abruptly.

Except for the unfortunate chap up in the crow's nest who clearly hadn't seen the signal. The sailor broke off after an awkward peal of lonely laughter.

Reva wondered if they had to practice this unusual arrangement. Rency seemed like the sort of captain who would rehearse the ridiculous.

Rency shot the crow's nest a foul look before stretching languidly and rubbing his stomach. "What time is it? I'm ready for breakfast. Anyone else hungry?" His hand reached into his trouser pocket.

"I'm hungry for blood," Isla said darkly.

Rency froze, but he wasn't looking at Isla and her pilfered cutlass. Instead he patted the front of his half-laced tunic and dug his fingers into the various pockets on his long coat. "Hey!" he said. "Where's my watch? Who took my watch?"

No one spoke.

Rency glared about the deck, narrowing his gaze on Isla in particular. "Don't look at me," she said, stabbing the point of the cutlass into the deck and leaning against the handle. "I only steal weapons. And kisses."

She shot a look over her shoulder and winked toward Reva, who laughed despite herself.

"Stop stabbing my ship." Rency launched forward and jostled Isla to the side so that he could snatch the cutlass away while she was distracted. "And if I find out who took my pocket watch, I'll have them drawn and quartered."

He tossed the cutlass toward one of the sailors. The fellow tried to catch it out of the air but missed and sent it clattering across the deck. With a sheepish glance over his shoulder, the pirate chased after the weapon and returned it to his belt. Is that who Ilsa had pilfered it from to begin with?

Several of the crew shouted promises to find the missing watch and dispersed in a thunder of boots against wood. While Rency was distracted, Reva glanced across the deck at Jareth to see how he was reacting. He nibbled on his lower lip, staring up at the crow's nest while rocking back and forth on the heels of his bare feet.

Something wiggled in one of the sea elf's coat pockets. A bright pink tentacle shot out briefly before disappearing from view. Calix? Or the other one?

She pursed her lips to hide a smile, somehow not surprised that Rency's crew had not only managed to kidnap an additional royal but also a nursery of baby krakens. How many did Jareth have stashed in those pockets of his?

The crew tore about the deck looking in the most ridiculous places for the missing watch. One chubby fellow with an eye patch even searched his own filthy pockets, piling various odds and ends on the barrel beside him. Rency stomped about, poking into things, muttering curses, and shooting Reva foul looks as if she were to blame, and Reva braced herself for more arguing, more shouting, and possibly more threats of dueling. But no one else noticed anything amiss with Jareth.

"Oy, Captain!" a sailor shouted from the crow's nest. "Shadow in the water!"

Rency, who'd begun to help the sailor with the eye patch empty his pockets, snapped his head around.

"What sort of shadow?" he shouted back. "How big?"

"I dunno!" said the crewman. "It's unnatural, Cap'n! It's an omen! We're doomed!"

"Oh, shut up!" Rency strode to the railing and looked in the direction the superstitious pirate was pointing. "Someone get me a spyglass!"

Reva started to follow but felt a hand snatch her arm. She paused as Jareth peered down at her, his expression dark.

"Wait. It could be dangerous."

Isla moved to join them, but she was watching Rency.

"What sort of danger?" Reva asked, pulling against Jareth's hold until he released her. "It's probably just a whale coming up for air. Unless…"

The problem in the cove.

"Pirates wouldn't get in a dither because of a whale," Isla said with a frown.

"Many creatures lurk in these waters." Jareth's voice held a pinched edge. "Dangerous creatures."

Reva couldn't argue with him because he *was* the prince of the sea elves.

He would know.

And he *had* said there was something in the cove…was that something following them?

"Unfurl all sails." Rency's voice rolled across the deck. "All hands on deck. *Andromeda*?" Rency looked toward the steering and lifted a hand. "Put on more speed. Make for Seriposa like your timbers are burning!"

"Why is he talking to the ship?" Isla whispered, taking a step closer to Reva. "Is he mad?"

"Yes. You're only now realizing that?"

Isla shot Reva a quelling look that soon twisted into a smile. But her humor faded as something arched out of the waves. Something dark, something huge…

"What is that?" Reva ignored the warnings of her companions and dashed to the ship's rail, leaning over to stare behind the *Andromeda*. Jareth and Ilsa pressed against her on either side. The wind tried to whip Rency's hat from her head, but Jareth clamped a hand down on the crown and pinned it in place for her.

"That's no whale," Isla said. She gripped the rail with both hands, leaning to see around Reva. "It's massive."

"Whatever it is, I don't think it's something we want to catch up to us." Jareth, still holding on to Reva's hat, reached into his pocket and withdrew one of his kraken babies. Holding it to his lips he whispered something Reva couldn't hear over the thunder of waves against the hull and the bellow of pirate voices.

Then he leaned over the railing and released the kraken. Reva gasped. How could he be so cruel? The baby kraken was so small, and they were up so high… But the kraken latched its suckers against the hull of the ship and slithered down the side of the *Andromeda* like a snake down a vine. With an unimpressive splash, he disappeared into the frothing waves.

With his arm around her to hang on to her hat, Reva almost felt as if he were hugging her. He stood so close. Memories of the previous night flooded her thoughts— memories of drowning and kissing and holding him beneath the waves.

Instead of being embarrassed by her wayward thoughts, she embraced them. As Jareth's sea-green eyes stared back at her, she couldn't escape the niggling thought…

What if Jareth turned out to be another Rency? Another stab in the back when she least expected it?

Rency was concerned Felix was the one who couldn't be trusted. But no one here could vouch for Jareth. No one but her. And what was her confidence based on?

His magical lips?

Her gaze dropped to that strangely gifted part of his face.

"What is it?" As his mouth formed the words, she tore her gaze back to his eyes, heat flooding her face.

"Where'd you send him?" she asked. "The baby. Where did you send him?"

Jareth quirked a smile. "I sent him to get help."

Reva turned back to watch the dark shape hulking beneath the waves as it gained on them with alarming speed. A sense of foreboding, of dread, filled her body. Judging by the tense atmosphere, the curses, the broken prayers and pleas to gods and divinities, she was not the only one who sensed the impending danger.

"I hope that blob of yours can swim really fast," Isla said, an edge in her voice. "I have a feeling we're going to need this help of which you speak."

Just then, a shudder tore through the *Andromeda,* and the crew began to scream.

Writhing black tentacles rose out of the sea alongside the *Andromeda.*

Reva gasped as Jareth and Isla tore her away from the railing. The wind caught Reva's hat and whipped it off her head. Isla slammed her hard into the main mast, while Jareth put himself between her and the black, snakish object rising over their heads. His back pressed hard into the arm Reva braced against his shoulders.

Horror and fear rippled through her as Reva tilted her head to watch the tentacle that rose higher, dousing them in water.

"Now!" Rency roared.

The *Andromeda* jolted with an unexpected burst of speed. A boom shook the planks beneath their feet. Sailors shouted as the huge arm blew apart in a puff of smoke and disappeared. Black blood splattered across the deck.

The arm about to crash across the ship had simply vanished.

"Did you see that?" Isla said, jumping up and down and pointing. "Pearls and cannonballs, did you see that?"

A tentacle flanked in suckers spun out of the water on the ship's aft, lashing out with powerful snaps.

The arm swept toward the deck. One of the sailors screamed and scrambled to avoid the plunging appendage, but he moved too slowly. The arm swept him clean off the deck and into the sea. His cutlass clattered to the deck.

"Man overboard!" Isla shouted, abandoning her post at Reva's side and dashing to the railing.

Another tentacle shot out of the sea—rising up, up over the deck of the ship above Isla. Reva screamed and pushed against Jareth, but he refused to move, keeping her pinned in place.

"Isla!" she shouted in warning.

But Isla was too focused on finding the sailor who'd been swept overboard to notice the danger arching up behind her.

CHAPTER TEN

Reva shoved Jareth as hard as she could and dove across the deck, scrambling on all fours until her fingers brushed the hilt of the sailor's discarded cutlass. She came up on one knee and swung the blade in an arc as the shadowy limb dropped straight toward her and Isla. Water rained down on her, and she screamed as she cut into the tentacle. Smoke, shadow, and inky black blood exploded around her.

A stench as foul as a rotting corpse forced its way into her nostrils and Reva coughed, gagging as she staggered to her feet. Jareth grabbed her wrist, yelling something into her face that she couldn't understand. She batted her free hand in front of her nose to clear the foul air.

"Do you have a death wish?" Jareth's voice finally cut through the fog of smoke and death.

"Not particularly. Why do you think I attacked the—the—what is this thing?" She wrenched her wrist from his grasp and searched the deck for Isla, hoping against hope that she hadn't also been knocked into the water. But the first mate still stood at the rail, splattered in black blood and seaspray but very much alive.

The *Andromeda* shuddered as two more tentacles sliced from the waves and slammed against the hull of the ship. The ship groaned, the timbers creaking against the force of the blow.

"Fire! Fire, you addlepated nincompoops!" Rency yelled over the din, his sailors ricocheting back and forth as if they hadn't a clue what they should be doing. "Fire everything! Just—just shoot at something! *Andromeda*, get us out of here!"

As the canons boomed and more tentacles disintegrated into smoke and black liquid, the ship screeched and plunged eastward, plowing through the waves. Reva stepped backward to catch her balance but tripped on the too long hem of Rency's ridiculous dress. She hit the deck hard on her rump and lost her grip on the cutlass.

"Reva! Are you hurt?"

Jareth bent to help her. One of his pockets writhed in frantic agitation, tiny pink arms spilling through the opening as Calix squelched out and dove for Reva. She caught him in both hands and let Jareth grab her by the elbows and tug her to her feet.

"I'm fine. I just tripped on this sea-forsaken dress—"

"Ahoy!" the sailor said from the crow's nest. "There are more of the beasties, Captain! Scores of the blighters!"

Still cradling the baby kraken in her palms, Reva pressed alongside Jareth at the railing as she searched the sea for signs of more attacking monsters.

"Don't shoot!" Jareth shouted. "They're coming to help! They're with me! Do *not* shoot!"

Calix wailed and wrapped his tentacles around Reva's fingers, squeezing so hard she thought she might lose feeling in her fingertips.

Rency, from the forecastle, waved his spyglass at Jareth. "Are you sure those things are on our side?"

"I'm sure!" Jareth jabbed a finger toward a frothing disturbance in the water. "Do *not* shoot my krakens, Rency!"

Rency jumped down to the lower deck and dashed toward them. He stopped on the other side of Isla, who shied away from him. Rency didn't notice. "If you're wrong, Magic Lips, no one will be alive to toss you overboard." He pressed the spyglass to his eye.

"Well?" Isla demanded. "What's happening? The monster has stopped attacking. For now."

"Aye." Rency squinted into the eye glass but didn't answer her question.

Growling with irritation, Isla snatched the eye glass from him, punching out half—heartedly with one arm when Rency tried to wrest his spy glass back.

"Oy, Reva!" Isla shouted. "They're attacking the black one! It's a battle of krakens, I tell you! Take a look at this—"

"I would if you'd give me back the glass!" Rency wrenched the spy glass from her hands.

By now, however, the battle had moved close enough that everyone could see the bubbling sea and explosions of black, pink, and dark maroon tentacles.

Reva clutched little Calix to her chest and stared at the adult krakens who'd come to the aid of the *Andromeda*. A huge portion of the sea bubbled like boiling water, tentacles exploding and slamming back into the waves as the krakens shrieked and roared. She'd never seen or heard anything like it in all her days. Not in any of the books in the Royal Library that she'd been forced to endure during her lessons.

"Why are they helping us?" Rency asked.

"I sent for them," Jareth answered. "Please don't shoot them. They're here to help."

Rency shot him a sharp look. "How do I know they won't turn on us the moment they've conquered the big one?"

"Have faith, Captain," Reva tried to intervene.

"You'll find I possess an astounding lack of faith in mankind," the captain growled.

Pushing back from the railing, Rency knocked into Isla in his haste to reach the mast of the ship.

"*Andromeda*," he said, "get us away from these krakens. Turn toward—"

But he was never able to say where the ship should turn. The *Andromeda* shuddered fiercely, like a dog shaking itself. Reva and those closest to her grabbed onto the railing to right themselves. Others, like Rency, were not as fortunate, and wound up being dropped mercilessly to the deck.

Reva stuffed Calix into her pocket and gripped the rail with both hands in case the ship lurched again.

"Don't you argue with me, ship!" Rency shouted as he leaped to his feet. He kicked the mast. "You turn this rotten pile of planks—"

The ship turned, alright, but not away from the krakens. Instead, she surged closer to the beasts trying to battle the giant monster who'd risen from the depths. Another huge black tentacle surged from the water and plummeted down on several dark red krakens trying to coil around one of its limbs.

"No, no, no!" Rency kicked the mast again. "You're going the wrong way. *Andromeda,* please…"

Isla snickered. "I've never heard a man quarrel with a ship like he would his wife," she said.

Reva was more interested in how the *ship* knew what Rency was saying to her and how she was *reacting* as if she were a living creature and not a thing of plank and sail.

"I don't think this is a normal ship." Her knuckles whitened as they curled more tightly around the railing.

"You're only now figuring that out?" Isla asked with a sideways glance. "Reva, you're slacking."

"I didn't *just* figure it out." Reva frowned at her, the tension in her body easing now that the krakens had drawn away the attacking monster. "I just didn't say anything until now because—because—"

"Because you thought you were going crazy?" Jareth asked. "That might be the reason I haven't said anything either. This ship likes my krakens. Apparently, it's a better judge of character than Rency."

The commotion beneath the waves subsided as the ship drew closer. The water, stained black from the blood of the mysterious beast, settled into a gentle roll.

"I think it's over," Reva said, searching for signs of the underwater battle renewing. She glimpsed shadows passing beneath the ship, but they were too small to be the beast. "Are those your krakens I see?"

"Yes." Jareth leaned beside her and waved to one of the shadows. A dark maroon tentacle shot out of the water and slapped playfully at the waves.

Behind them, Rency gave an exasperated howl. "I yield! Do what you want. You always do!"

Reva turned to watch as Rency threw himself down beside the mast, legs sprawling like he'd expended every last speck of his strength arguing with his magical ship. The *Andromeda* skipped across the waves like a lamb happily frolicking in an open pasture.

"Be kind to your ship, Rency!" Reva called, unable to help herself. Both Isla and Jareth succumbed to fits of laughter. Even Calix wiggled and purred in her pocket.

"Foul, vile vessel," Rency said. "One day I'll chop her up, plank by plank, and feed her to the flames. See if I don't."

Reva shook her head. "I wonder why you didn't choose a less quarrelsome ship. One would think a pliable ship is a must for a pirate."

"Merchant sailor," he bawled at her. "I'm a *merchant* sailor! Not a pirate. Not a kidnapper. I saved your life, Reva Morrigan. If you'd stayed at Black Rock, you'd be dead right now."

His head fell back against the mast as he stared up into the taut white sails. "I saved your life." These last words dropped so low Reva strained to catch them.

She shot a questioning look at Isla. "Say something nice?" Isla whispered with a cocked eyebrow and a shrug.

Reva grimaced and moved over to Rency. After a moment's hesitation, she sat cross-legged across from him and braced her hands against her exposed knees. "All right," she said in a gentler tone. "I'm sorry I cut up your mother's dress."

Rency sniffed woundedly and refused to look at her.

She drummed her fingers against her knees and tried again. "I'm sorry your ship is so… disobedient."

Calix hiccupped in her pocket, and Rency narrowed his eyes.

"I'm sorry I called you a pirate. And I'm sorry if you thought it was a good idea to lure me onto the sea and *forcibly* drag me into your cabin."

A smile tugged at his mouth. "I slept in the crew quarters, I'll have you know. It was abysmal."

"So why *did* you do it? Kidnap—I mean—*rescue me.*"

Rency heaved a long-suffering sigh, and Reva braced herself for the most exaggerated sob story she'd ever had the misfortune to hear. "Why did I do it, Reva? I should think that was obvious by now."

"Well, it isn't obvious to me. So spell it out, Rency. Please."

"That dress looks good on you, you know. Even with it…tattered. It shows off your lovely legs—"

"Rency." She growled the word low in her throat, balling her hands into fists.

Behind her, Jareth suffered from another violent fit of coughing. Rency shot him a smug look before turning back to Reva.

"Fine. I should think it was obvious that Prince Felix—your most *uncharming* suitor—is trying to take control of Etthan by having you assassinated."

Ripples passed over Reva's flesh at the thought, but she didn't think Felix had the brains to pull off an assassination attempt like this. Not on his own. And that meant one of two things…either the king of Desta wanted her dead or…

She shivered as if from a bone-chilling cold. She didn't want to consider that Cassandra was making a play for the throne. The thought made her sick.

Fingers touched Reva's shoulder moments before Jareth crouched beside her. Behind him, Isla had also moved to stand closer. "What makes you think Felix was responsible for the attack on the beach?" he asked quietly.

Rency frowned at him, bending one knee so he could brace his bare forearm against it. "Oh, *please*. Who else did you think it could have been?"

"You." Jareth's voice held no mercy but no genuine accusation either.

"If Rency wanted her dead, he's had ample opportunities to make it happen," Isla said. The sick expression on her face suggested it rankled every bone in her body to have to admit it out loud.

Reva sucked on her lower lip and tried to pull together her confused thoughts.

"Thank you for that, Isla." Rency pressed one palm against his chest. "That means the world to me."

Jareth snorted. "I still am not convinced Felix is the villain in this. Why would he blow up his own ship? Have either of you considered that?"

"I don't think he did," Reva said, thinking about her next words. "At least, not on his own."

Silence hung among them as the others absorbed her words. "So, what are you saying?" Rency said with exaggerated emphasis on each word, "that the explosion on the *Endellion* and the attack on your own person were executed by two separate parties? For two entirely different agendas?" He did nothing to mask his scorn or disbelief.

Licking her lips, she looked across the deck at the crew who'd already begun cleanup and repairs after the attack. "No, I don't think that," she said carefully. "It's too much of a coincidence. But our list of suspects has narrowed uncomfortably. And while I don't see why Felix would destroy his own ship, it's obvious he isn't working alone."

"As we've already established, I've had ample opportunities to do you in…and I haven't," Rency said woundedly. "I am the hero in this sordid tale, not the villain."

Isla barked a laugh, but there wasn't anything humorous in the sound. "That's not what she's saying, you fools."

Reva leaned back to study her friend's face. They exchanged a long, measured look, and Reva wondered if Isla had begun to suspect what Reva had.

"Well, it wasn't me," Jareth said quietly. "I would die before I let anyone hurt you, Reva."

His words sent a new wave of shivers across Reva's skin. Their kiss beneath the sea was beginning to develop nuances she wasn't sure she was prepared to deal with.

"Isn't that sweet?" Rency rolled his eyes toward the skies. "Don't forget—I've also taken great pains to protect you, Reva."

It took every ounce of self-control she possessed not to punch him in the face. "Forgive me if I don't feel any sympathy for *your* pains."

Now Jareth on the other hand…

Her cheeks still burned from his ardent declaration. Truth? Or a clever ploy to earn her trust?

Was it possible that Jareth actually cared about her? As more than a princess he hoped to marry for political gain? She'd always scoffed at stories about heroes and damsels in distress falling in love at first sight. It was the stuff of fairy tales.

And yet…she could not deny *something* tugged her toward Jareth, something she had never felt for anyone before. Was it something inside her, something that had been searching for a companion soul? Or was it the power of sea magic?

"What of the attack on my ship? My poor, innocent, darling ship." Rency kissed his fingertips and then patted the deck beside him. A rumble of—was that pleasure? —creaked the timbers of the *Andromeda*. "Doesn't this prove I am also a victim? Perhaps they were trying to assassinate *me*."

Jareth and Reva snorted in unison, exchanging awkwardly amused smiles afterward.

"No, you nincompoop," Isla said, stepping closer to kick Rency hard on the thigh.

He yelped and raked her with a foul look.

"You're not listening to her," Isla said as she jabbed a finger toward Reva. "She doesn't think you or Jareth have anything to do with this. And she doesn't think Felix is working alone. So do your sums, pirate."

Reva held her breath and waited for Rency to put the pieces together. Jareth shifted his gaze between them, looking confused. But it only took a moment for the annoyance to leak out of Rency's expression, replacing it with something somber.

"You think he's working with Cassandra. But she's such a—" He hesitated and scratched behind his ear and searched for words.

"A conniving witch?" Isla suggested grimly.

Reva winced but couldn't argue with her friend. Cassandra had always played the part of spoiled courtier, but she was more than that. "But," she said, "this doesn't explain the sea monster who attacked the *Andromeda*."

"It's not a sea monster," Jareth said. His tone was low, and when she looked up into his face, his sea-green eyes were piercing. "I don't know what it is, but that thing doesn't come from the sea."

A fist tightened inside her stomach. "What do you mean?"

"It wasn't the usual sort of sea monster. This was something else. Something worse."

"What could be worse than a gigantic kraken trying to rip my ship apart?" Rency asked, his voice rising and eliciting concerned glances from the crew.

Jareth hesitated and leaned closer to Rency, as if he didn't want the crew to hear him. "Someone used an artifact to summon this creature—an unnatural creature. And I think *you* might know what sort of object could do such a thing." Jareth patted the deck of the ship. "You already have more than your fair share of *unnatural* possessions, Rency."

He was referring to the *Andromeda*, naturally. Rency's magical pirate ship.

"Are you saying *I* summoned the kraken—monster—thing?" Rency's voice dripped with dislike.

"No," Reva said with a meaningful look at Jareth, "but I noticed black ink in the water around the *Endellion*. And today, when we fought the monster, didn't you notice how it exploded and left behind a liquid substance—something like blood that wasn't blood? Something like *ink?*"

As if to prove her point, a sailor waltzed by with a mop, cleaning up the black residue from the deck.

"I noticed," Rency said darkly, staring at her with unsettling intensity. He stroked his goatee with one hand and mulled her words over before continuing, "Well, I don't personally have any experience with such things…but this could be the work of a Death Pearl."

Jareth sucked in a startled breath, and Reva frowned at him. By the sands, what was a Death Pearl? And why did the mention of it make Jareth look like he'd seen a ghost?

Reva studied them each in turn, frowning. "What's a Death Pearl?"

"It's dark magic—the forbidden arts," Rency whispered. "A relic from before the formation of the islands—before Etthan. Before Seriposa. Even before Desta."

"From the Dark Elf war that tore Rhuin apart," Jareth said in a hushed voice. "My people suffered much in the war."

Reva frowned as she searched her memories for the lessons she'd been forced to study on ancient history. "We *all* suffered in that war," she pointed out. "We all sacrificed. Everyone did. That's how our island realms were formed. Humans fled the Dark War and took to the seas in search of a new home. But that was 500 years ago. What does that have to do with us? With now?"

Rency raked her with a condescending glare. "My dear child, the dark elves used weapons in the war that nearly destroyed the world."

"Death pearls." Jareth rested a hand over hers and searched her eyes as if looking for answers. "They've been lost all these centuries. But my people still tell the stories of the Trident. Of the magic that was stolen from our waters to wage the dark elf war."

"Aye," Rency said, "and the sirens paid dearly to regain their magic."

Jareth dipped his head as if to thank him for the admission.

"And you think someone is stealing magic again?"

Rency shook his head. "No. The Trident was lost long ago. The magic returned to the sea."

"But if someone has found a pearl…"

Reva's blood ran cold at the somber tone in Jareth's words. A premonition of something horrific pressed down on her shoulders. "If someone has found one of these death pearls, we could all be in danger."

"Not just the islands," Rency said without emotion. "All of Rhuin."

CHAPTER ELEVEN

ll of Rhuin.

Surely, he wasn't implying that they were on the edge of another war. Her people were already starving. She needed to secure trade routes…not lead her people into a battle that would rip away the last vestiges of their resources.

"I can't allow war," she whispered, the blood draining from her face. "My people wouldn't survive it. We don't stand a chance."

Neither of them answered her, but Jareth's fingers tightened over hers, and even Rency's playful eyes darkened with understanding. It hurt making such a declaration—admitting that her kingdom and her people were so vulnerable. They were truly at the mercy of the highest bidder, and Reva's hand was in the balance.

Somehow it always came back to this.

But if Cassandra and Felix were working together against her…how could she fight them both? She was exposed on all fronts, without enough information to come up with a plan. She didn't know who was the mastermind in this coup, who was controlling the dark magic that had already taken the lives of Felix's crew and could come for her people next…

As much as she wanted to keep herself out of danger, she couldn't think like that.

Reva took a bracing breath. "I-I need to return to Black Rock."

Jareth and Rency exploded into denial simultaneously, but Reva threw away Jareth's hand and jumped to her feet, hands on her hips.

"I am returning to Black Rock," she said, her voice echoing across the deck of the ship. "I am Princess Reva Morrigan, heir to the throne of Etthan, and I command you to return me to my ship!"

The authority in her voice left a startled calm in its wake. Jareth and Rency both stood to face her, their expressions mutinous. This wasn't a battle she'd win without a fight. She glared at first Rency, then Jareth, and then back to the pirate captain. With no thought of the consequences, she took a menacing step toward him and pointed her finger into his face.

"You," she breathed, her body trembling, "will take me back."

Rency's mouth thinned into a taut line, his nostrils flaring. "I will not. Not when I worked so hard to save your life the first time."

Reva spun to face Jareth. "Then *you* will take me back."

Contrary to Rency's defiance, Jareth practically melted with horror and misery. "I can't, Reva! I'd be taking you back just to let you die! You need to think clearly about this."

"I am. I can't hide on this ship and avoid my duties. Every minute I am here, *they* are scheming behind my back and taking my island from me. And I can guarantee you the well-being of my people isn't high on their list of priorities."

"So what? You're just going to hand yourself over to them for execution?" Isla asked, disbelief twisting her words. She stepped around Jareth and Rency and grabbed Reva by the arm. "Have you gone mad?"

"*No.*" Reva ground her teeth together and willed *someone* to support her in this. Anyone. "They don't know that I suspect them, or that we know about the dark magic. And as loath as I am to say it, I still need Felix. I need his trade routes. I need *food*. And if a war is coming, I need to make alliances that will protect Etthan."

"So you're just going to roll over and give up?" Rency asked. "Sell your freedom for a loaf of bread?"

That blade dug deep into her heart.

Oh no, she thought hopelessly. *I'll be selling much more than that.*

"I need more information," she said, her voice hitching. She cleared her throat before continuing. "And I can't get that here. Maybe I can turn Felix to my side—or Cassandra. One of them might be coerced to see reason."

Rency snorted.

"And if not," Reva continued, glaring at him, "then I'll do what I have to do. For Etthan."

Jareth must have seen something in her eyes because his face went slack. "You'll marry Felix," he rasped, "even knowing what he is. What he's done."

Her traitorous heart rose in her throat, and a part of her hated him for entering her life just to make this decision harder. "Yes."

"But you can't!"

"It's my choice. When the time comes…it will be my sacrifice to make for my people."

Rency barked a laugh, but it wasn't one of mirth. Instead, it was filled with derision. "No, you misunderstand, love. You *can't* marry Felix, not truly. Don't you know why sailors are so afraid of being lured into the water by the lovely lasses beneath the waves?" He pursed his lips and made kissing noises.

Reva had too much pride to admit that she didn't, nor did she understand what this had to do with Felix.

"Because," Rency said without pity, "there is power in a siren's kiss."

"I know that: I didn't drown, now, did I?" Impatience made her words sharp and angry.

Jareth turned his back on them. She didn't like the way he ran his hand over the back of his head, the way he let it linger on his neck as if he were in pain, as if something were bothering him.

"Oh, aye," Rency said. "It does that. But it does a whole lot more as well. Tell her, Magic Lips. Tell her what you did when you plucked her from the waves so heroically."

Jareth's spine stiffened, his shoulders going taut beneath the leathers and bits of silver armor. He turned his face so she could see the curve of his cheek, the flutter of his eyelashes as he stared down at the deck. "I saved her life," he said quietly.

"Not that bit, mate. Tell her the rest of it."

What else was there for her to know?

Still Jareth didn't answer. He wouldn't look at her, and that more than anything made her realize her fears had proven true. There was more to this elvish prince—secrets he hadn't told her, secrets that would probably only cause her pain.

"What is he talking about?" she asked around the lump in the back of her throat. "What did you do to me, Jareth?"

"I saved your life."

"No. What did you *do* to me?"

He turned just enough so that he could look at her, but his posture reminded her of a wild animal cornered by a predator. Was his secret so terrible?

"I bound you to the sea, Reva Morrigan," he said, each syllable laced with pain. "I bound you to me."

Her heartbeat stuttered and then pounded more quickly. *But what does that mean?* She wanted to hurl the words at him, but she kept her face expressionless, waiting for him to continue.

"There is a reason sailors fear the siren's kiss." He shifted to face her head on. "Because those who experience it are never the same. If they try to return to their homes, they go mad with longing for the sea. And for the woman they left behind in the waters."

"Or the boy, in this case," Rency said.

Reva shot him a quelling look, but for once he didn't look as if he meant to poke fun at her. Instead, he looked weary to the bone.

"I'm not bewitched," she said, still focused on Rency. "I am in complete control of my faculties."

"Oh, aye, love, I'm not saying you've lost your mind. I'm saying you're *going* to lose it if you try to turn your back on your little siren prince. The Sea Song will call you back, no matter how far you try to run. And that's not the worst of it."

"There's more?" She couldn't keep the stunned horror out of her voice.

"Rency." The sea pirate's name on Jareth's lips held a note of warning. "She's heard enough."

"Oh, I don't think so. She's just getting warmed up, aren't you, Reva? Tell him you want to—"

"Oy, Captain!" someone bawled from up in the rigging. "Ship on the horizon!"

Rency's head snapped back, and he launched himself toward the forecastle. "Which one?"

"I can't tell—wait! She's flyin' the flag of Etthan, Captain! It's the *Perseus!*"

Reva had hoped the sighting of her flagship meant this nightmare was nearly over, that Cassandra had sent Captain Dren to bring her home. But Rency wasn't the self-proclaimed prince of pirates for nothing. He knew his way about the seas—and when he was getting along with his ship, he seemed unstoppable.

Somewhere in the outskirts of Seriposa, he successfully lost the *Perseus*. Using the small islands and dangerous shoals to both obscure and hinder pursuit, Rency guided the *Andromeda* out of sight.

Reva stood at the window in the captain's cabin, hoping against hope that Captain Dren would see through Rency's trickery, but night fell, and no more sails appeared on the horizon.

Something soft and moist pressed against her wrist. She looked down to see Calix peeking out of her pocket, his eyes on her as if asking a question. She smiled and patted him on the head with two fingers. "I'm okay, little fellow."

But she wasn't.

He burrowed back into her pocket, purring so loud she could feel the vibrations against her thigh.

A knock echoed from the hallway, but she ignored it and remained at her post. But her unwanted guest persisted until she barked an irritable, "Well, let yourself in then! The door isn't locked!"

The door creaked open, and feet thumped against the floorboards. She turned to cast a scathing remark at her captor, but it wasn't Rency's swaggering form that filled the doorway.

It was Jareth.

She whipped her face back to the port hole, her heart hurting at the sight of him. "I don't want to see you," she said quietly. "Please, leave me."

"Reva, we need to talk." He sounded haggard, and under other circumstances she may have felt pity for him. But he didn't deserve her pity.

"I have nothing to say to you. I've made up my mind, Jareth. I'm going home, one way or another."

Wood creaked behind her, and she imagined him gripping the back of the chair, leaning his weight against it. "You may have nothing to say to me, but I have more to say to you. I need you to understand why I used the siren kiss on you."

"I know why. You saw me in a moment of vulnerability and took advantage of my weakness. You used my accident to try to steal my throne."

"I don't want your throne, Reva. I never wanted that."

She braced her forearm against the wall and stared out into the black night. The hiss and low roar of the ocean rose from beyond the small hole in the wall of the ship. "What else could you want? Why else did you crawl out of the sea and ruin my attempts to save my people?"

"Because…because you aren't the only one trying to save his people."

Her breath hitched in her throat.

His people.

She didn't miss the use of the masculine possessive. Still, she remained frozen at the window, her spine rigid and unyielding. Whatever his excuse, it didn't give him the right to bind her to him without permission. What kind of a monster did that?

He was as bad as Rency—perhaps worse.

"My kingdom is on the precipice of destruction," he said more quietly. "I was sent to save them. You were my hope for salvation, Reva. In you, I saw a future for both our peoples. Side by side."

She turned then, slowly, her fingers trailing down the wall and falling idle at her side. He stood just as she had imagined, shoulders hunched as his hands gripped the back of the chair. "What threatens your people, Jareth?"

He wouldn't meet her gaze, focused on the tabletop before him. "Old age," he said with a bitter laugh. "Old age and old prejudices."

She held her breath as he lifted his head to look at her. In his youthful eyes, made midnight blue by the dimness of the cabin, she saw someone much older. Someone, like her, who carried heavy burdens, ones much too heavy to bear.

Yet neither of them had a choice to walk away from their burdens. Too many people depended on them.

Too many kingdoms.

"Old age?" she asked as she crossed the room and seated herself on Rency's chair with a heavy sigh. She motioned for him to sit as well. "You might need to explain."

He exhaled slowly and straightened. Instead of pulling out the chair, however, he held one hand out to her. "If you don't mind, I'd prefer to walk the deck. Walls make me…nervous."

Reva hesitated and bit her lip. She would have preferred to have this difficult conversation with the safety of a table between them. But if walking would help him open up and answer her questions, she could work with that. So she shoved back her chair and circled the table.

She left his hand hanging in the air, however, and stalked from the cabin unaccompanied.

Jareth followed her in silence.

The *Andromeda,* too, was quiet with the crew either in their bunks or at the lookouts. To make sure the ship remained hidden in the cove, the lanterns had been shuttered or extinguished. Reva searched the shadows around the quarterdeck but saw no sign of Rency or Isla.

"So." She cleared her throat and glanced up at the sea elf. "Old age?"

"It's difficult to explain to a human." He matched her whisper with one of his own. "Your world is one of science and logic. Of tangible things you can see and touch."

"Your world isn't?"

He braced his forearms against the railing and smiled out at the darkness. "No, Reva, it isn't."

She waited for him to continue.

"The magic that keeps my kingdom safe is dying. The mother kraken…is dying."

"Kraken?" Reva echoed in surprise. "That's where your magic comes from?"

He shifted to press his hip against the railing. "No, Reva, she provides us a haven in her realm. Our magic is of the sea."

"But…she's dying? The mother kraken?"

"Yes. Calypso is dying. And when she dies, the magic that keeps my world intact will splinter. The streets will flood, and my people will be lost to the waters we love so much."

"Then swim away and find some new place to live."

A cloud passed over the crescent moon and cast Jareth's face into deeper shadows. "It doesn't work that way, I'm afraid. Some of us would survive. But the little ones…they can't control the magic of the sea yet. And the old and the infirm…we would never have time to save them all."

"Then evacuate before the kraken dies."

He took a step closer, reaching for her so suddenly she only had time to gasp before he caught her elbows in both hands. "Reva," he said tightly, "that's what I'm trying to do! My people need a new home. We need some place to go. No one else will take us in. There are too many memories, too much bad blood between our peoples. *You* are my only hope, Reva."

Sand and pearls! He stood so close, staring down at her with such agonizing earnestness she couldn't look away.

"I will do what I can for your people, Jareth. But I can't marry you. Etthan cannot support refugees. Our own future is so uncertain…"

"We'd be able to help your people. Teach them to fish in the best places. Use our magic to grow crops. Bring food from the sea. We have ways."

"It would be too little, too late, I'm afraid." She didn't know why, but her gaze fell to his mouth. It was a very nice mouth. Beautifully formed and surrounded by a scruff of dark whiskers that she found unaccountably attractive. *Curse his magical mouth…*

"It's our only hope, Reva," he whispered, every word laced with a desperation she knew all too well. He leaned closer. To peer into her eyes? Or…

Was he going to kiss her again?

She gasped and shied away, spinning so her back was to the railing and she was facing the deck.

"Don't touch me, Jareth," she said, but her voice trembled, filling her with embarrassment. She hoped he couldn't hear the furious pounding of her heart.

"Reva, please—"

"No." She stiffened her spine. "You've had your fun with me, and now we must pay the price—whatever that price entails. I will leave the sea and return to my people, and you will return to yours. I'll do what I can for your little ones and elderly. But that's all."

She couldn't allow her heart to lead her astray. She had to do what was best for her people. If sacrificing herself in marriage to preserve the best trade routes—to avoid war—was what it took, that was what she would do. Because she was a princess, a daughter of kings. And no matter how she might wish to be a normal woman, who married a man for love rather than her kingdom's future, that was not up to her.

"So you'll turn me away, despite my promise to help your people, in favor of a man who neither knows nor cares for you."

Reva rubbed her forearms to dissipate the cold shiver that passed over her at the sad words. "Yes," she whispered. "That's about the sum of it."

"I, too, must do what is best for my people," Jareth said, spreading his hands. Fine hands, they were too. Large and strong, yet gentle enough to pet a baby kraken and tuck it away in a pocket for safekeeping.

Reva looked up, studying his face as the clouds shifted and cast cool white moonlight over his high cheekbones. She desperately wanted to find another solution, to listen to the whispers of her heart that said Jareth would make a more loyal husband and better king than Felix.

Felix who stood on the beach and let his people drown. Felix who might want her dead.

But Jareth had tricked her once, and she couldn't take the chance that there was more he hadn't told her. Tears pricked her eyes.

"I'm sorry, Jareth," she whispered. "But I cannot save your people *and* mine. It's too great a burden for one woman. I'm sorry."

His eyes rolled closed, and he heaved a painful sigh. Then, his eyes flew open, and he caught her by both elbows once again. "I'm sorry too," he whispered. "Hold your breath, Reva."

Before she had time to scream for help, Jareth had swept her into his arms, leaped onto the railing, and plunged them both over the side of the ship.

CHAPTER TWELVE

Reva's strangled cry cut short as the cold water closed over her head.

She'd barely registered the wild swirl of sensations, the stomach-wrenching plunge into deep darkness. The shock of ice-cold water against her skin. Jareth's arms wrapping around her like iron bars. The smothering saltwater forcing its way into her mouth and nose as he dragged her below the waves.

She kicked and struggled against his hold, but he was far too strong. Something coiled around her legs, and then her waist. Reva tried to scream but only choked on the sea water she swallowed.

Had he saved her only to murder her now?

This is it, her brain told her. *This is where you die. Your kingdom lost. Your people lost.* You *lost at sea.*

No! She had to fight, had to swim, had to…

But whatever had latched about her legs and waist only drew her deeper and deeper beneath the surface. She continued to choke, water overwhelming every one of her senses. The deepest blackness imaginable pressed in on her. Then Jareth found her mouth, his hands tangling in her hair.

And, sharks bite her, she let him kiss her. In her weakness, in her need to survive, she let him kiss her. She'd never felt more vulnerable, more helpless. Even her tears were stolen away by the sea.

But at least her lungs filled and emptied. At least life flooded through her veins. As they were dragged deeper into the ocean, Jareth wrapped one arm around her to hold her close. The thing dragging them down also wrapped around him. Why didn't he flinch away from the imprisonment of those arms crawling around them, those…tentacles?

Krakens.

The revelation sent a jolt of shock through her. She jerked backward, pulling her face away from Jareth's. Immediately, her lungs pressed in on her, as if the darkness were a fist squeezing the life from her chest. Jareth's free hand frantically pulled at her neck until he found her mouth again.

Let him breathe for you, she told herself. *No matter what happens, you need to live for your people. So let him breathe…just…breathe…*

She would find a way to escape. Again. No matter how endless this darkness seemed, it would not be the end of her. She would not always be a prisoner.

But even these repeated promises of strength and courage and freedom grew shallow as the kraken's arms wrapped her and Jareth in a cocoon she knew she could never break free of if she ever wanted to see the surface again.

Her world became nothing but darkness of the water, the power of the kraken's arms, and the warmth of the elf prince who'd betrayed her.

Reva jerked back to consciousness, rudely awakened by pain. Her body slid across a hard surface, Jareth's arms and legs entangled with hers. Water flowed around them, sucking at her hair and clothes as it sloshed and trickled away. His weight pressed down on her, his breathing loud and labored. He rolled to the side, freeing her, but the pressure in her lungs didn't ease.

And what of Calix? Was he being crushed in her pocket?

She gagged and inhaled a single, agonizing breath. Her chest *hurt*, like someone had been sitting on her ribcage, crushing her. Shadows and smears of light hung above her, too jumbled for her to figure out what she was looking at.

A hand found hers and squeezed.

"Just breathe through it," Jareth whispered into the half-light. "It'll pass."

He held tight to her fingers as she struggled to remember how to use her own lungs.

"I'm sorry." His voice washed over her like the waves still licking her arms and legs. "It happens when you're under water for more than a few minutes. Your body needs to remember how to breathe on its own. I'm sorry, Reva, I'm *so* sorry."

How could he do this to her? She wanted to scream and punch him in retaliation, but she choked and grappled for air. Her body writhed as it fought what had once been so easy.

She couldn't do this—couldn't remember—

Fingers stroked her brow and threaded into her hair. "Breathe, Reva. You need to breathe."

The pain was too much, too intense—

He kissed her temple and pressed his forehead to hers. "Please, Reva. You can't give up. Your people need you. We need you. And—" He choked off. "*I* need you."

Breath rattled into her constricted lungs. Jareth rolled her onto her side, holding her in place as sea water and bile burned the back of her throat. Calix wiggled out of her pocket, balancing on the curve of her hip and squeaking in agitation.

At least he hadn't been squashed to pulp.

Reva coughed so hard she feared she would spit out her own internal organs. She tried to ignore the hand rubbing between her shoulder blades and the voice whispering apologies into her ears.

How dare he?

"Leave me alone," she half-sobbed.

He froze, his words faltering into silence. Then his hands withdrew, and he left her alone on cold stone. She curled into a fetal position and tried to restrain the sobs begging to be released. She wouldn't cry. She couldn't fall apart, not yet.

There was so much she needed to do—so many people she had to be strong for.

And she hated Jareth for making her feel vulnerable. Somehow, his betrayal was worse than Rency's.

It hurt more because—despite her best efforts to remain practical—she wanted to trust Jareth, wanted him to be the answer to her problems.

Wanted him to save her.

She wanted to be the damsel in distress, not the heroine the world needed her to be. She wrapped one arm around her head and screamed soundlessly into a void nothing could penetrate. Ever since her father had died, she'd been forced to depend on herself. There hadn't been anyone else she could turn to. And then Jareth had come along and turned her world upside down. And she'd let him.

What would it have been like to have someone strong standing beside her? Holding her hand? Sharing her burdens?

She would never know.

Because some burdens could only be carried alone. Jareth wasn't the shining knight in the story books who swept in to save the helpless princess. He was the cretin who used her and left her heartbroken.

Her silent cries caught as she inhaled a ragged, determined breath. He couldn't save her *because she wasn't the helpless princess.*

She was Crown Princess of Etthan, the only heir of a dead king, and her people depended on her. She drew in another shuddering breath and blew it out slowly. Breathing became easier with every inhale and exhale. She scooped up Calix and shoved herself into a seated position, bracing one hand against the ground until the trembling subsided.

She could sense Jareth crouched beside her. Around them, water sloshed and echoed strangely against walls she couldn't see in the deep shadows. After sliding Calix back into her pocket, she stood and tested her wobbly legs. Water squished unpleasantly inside her boots and caused Rency's dress to cling to her body. She tried to squeeze out the skirt with shaking hands.

As she did, she swept her gaze up at the ceiling above them. They were in some sort of underwater grotto illuminated by ghostly blue light. It took her a moment to find the source of the light—it streamed from half a dozen holes in the ceiling and walls. Except, they weren't truly holes, for something kept the water from rushing into the grotto and drowning them. Reva took a tentative step toward the wall and stared through the window at the glowing creatures swimming just outside.

Jellyfish wafted past her and cast light against her damp cheeks. Mouth slightly ajar, Reva reached to touch the surface that hung suspended between her and the ocean. It wasn't hard like glass but gave slightly when she pressed against it.

"Where are we?" she whispered as the first jellyfish was joined by a smaller one.

Behind her, Jareth sighed heavily. "This is Argos," he said, his voice lacking all inflection. "I've brought you home."

As the jellyfish wafted beyond her viewpoint, Reva withdrew her fingers from the barrier. "This isn't home," she said quietly.

She waited for him to respond, but Jareth said nothing. At last, she turned to face him, even though he was the last person she wanted to look at right now. Voices echoed from deeper in the grotto. Sea-green lights flickered against the walls inside an opening at the opposite end of the chamber. Moments later, bright glowing orbs and shadowy figures appeared.

"Jareth, is that you?" a feminine voice called out.

The sea prince heaved a weighty sigh and tore his gaze from Reva's. "I'm here, Belen!" he called to the shadows.

A thin figure with a lantern peeled out of the darkness and moved to join them, illuminated by the glowing orb inside the metal casing. It was a young female elf with Jareth's long dark hair and piercing sea-green eyes. She wore a gown the color of shallow waters, clasped at one shoulder with a golden shell broach. Two more shadows appeared behind her—male guards carrying tridents and lanterns.

Reva pressed her back against the wall of the grotto and instinctively grasped for the knife she kept in her boot, only to remember that Rency had stolen it and never returned it.

Belen set her lantern on the ground and reached up to hug Jareth. While she looked about the same age as Reva, she was *tiny*, barely five feet tall. Jareth stooped down in order to hug her back. Their embrace lingered several moments before he withdrew.

"I'm so glad you've returned," she said, gripping his arm with a pale hand. "There was another breach this morning."

Jareth's gasp echoed through the grotto. "How many?" he asked, voice pained as the two guards drew closer and stopped on either side of the girl. One of them cast a curious look toward Reva.

"Three," the girl said, swiping at tears on her cheeks. "We tried to get to them, but there wasn't time to rescue everyone. I'm sorry, Jareth—they tried. They truly did."

His shoulders hunched, and the meaning of the girl's words finally dawned on Reva.

They were talking about people. They'd lost *people* that morning.

Her throat swelled. So Jareth hadn't been lying—at least not about all of it. His world really was crashing in around him, but that still hadn't given him the right to abduct her.

And yet…she pressed her back to the wall and felt trapped by the uncertainty. She couldn't be responsible for saving his people as well as her own. He asked too much. How would she feed them? She'd be saving them from the sea just to die a slower death on land.

"Reva?" Jareth's voice pulled her out of her frantic reverie.

"I'm sorry?" She licked her lips and took a stumbling step forward.

His eyebrows tugged together as he frowned at her, but he didn't voice the question in his gaze.

"Who is this?" Belen asked as Reva stepped into the circle of light cast by the lanterns—the ones lit not with wick and fire but by tiny schools of glowing fish in clear basins of water. "Is this—is this her?" Awe mingled with hope, and the look on Belen's face drove a blade into Reva's heart.

"I'd like you to meet my sister, Belen," Jareth said, still staring at Reva with uncertainty painted in his eyes.

Reva ignored the doubt in his gaze and the hope in his sister's and drew herself up as tall as could. In the center of the grotto at the bottom of the sea, she lifted her chin and fell back on her role of feral queen.

You can do this, you must *do this…*

"I am Crown Princess of Etthan," she said with as much coldness as she could dredge from her soul. "I was taken against my will, and I *demand* you return me to my people."

All color drained from the elf girl's face and replaced her curiosity and excitement with horror. She tore her gaze from Reva's and looked to Jareth instead. "Jareth," Belen choked, one hand lifting to rest on the white pearls circling her throat. "What have you done?"

Reva held herself immobile and waited for his excuses, for the feeble self-defense. But Jareth said nothing. He stood there, head bent and stooped shoulders, refusing to look at anyone. The seconds ticked by, and Reva waited. They all waited.

"Reva," he began, turning and reaching for her hand.

But she flinched and jerked backward. "Don't touch me!" She wrapped her arms around herself, shivering uncontrollably as he shrank away from her. His outstretched fingers curled into his palm.

Then, Jareth simply walked away. Reva watched him go, trying to ignore the stabbing pain in her heart. Her own words came back to haunt her.

Don't touch me. Leave me alone.

He was only doing what she'd told him to do.

Reva shivered uncontrollably as Jareth left the chamber. As soon as he disappeared from sight, a dam broke, and her strength abandoned her. She swayed as a driving desire to chase after him ran unbidden through her thoughts.

What was wrong with her?

Teeth chattering, Reva weaved back and forth.

Belen took her by the hand and said something. As warmth coursed up her arm and through her veins, Reva exhaled audibly. "Oh," she said as the tremors began to subside. "Thank you. That feels better."

The elf princess eyed her strangely and then bowed over Reva's hand. An uncomfortable feeling clawed inside Reva's chest as the elf girl slowly rose, her eyes downcast. "I'm sorry for my brother's foolishness," Belen said, her lips quivering. "He shouldn't have used the kiss on you."

How did Belen know about *that*? Reva glanced at the two guards, who had also dipped their heads differentially.

"He's—he's desperate, Your Highness," Belen said as she rose to her full height, as short as that was. She was barely five foot tall with her shoes on. "Most desperate. I know you have no reason to believe a word I say, but please believe me. He truly didn't mean you any harm by bringing you here."

Reva cleared her throat and let her hand fall back to her side where it rested against the pocket that contained a purring Calix. "Yes, he's mentioned a little of your troubles. I'm sorry. H-how could you tell he…kissed me?" Fire warmed her cheeks, but she fought to maintain her royal poise.

Belen's lips thinned then curved in a faint smile. "I can tell by looking at you," she whispered. "It's in the way you look at him."

"Excuse me? How *I* look at him?"

The elf girl's smile widened briefly before it faded completely. "Yes," she said uneasily. "And he looks at you the same way."

"And how is that?" Reva couldn't keep the bitterness from her tone.

"Like he's drowning without you."

CHAPTER
THIRTEEN

Belen's words twisted something into Reva's chest. Was this what Rency and Jareth had meant when they said she'd go mad with longing if she tried to leave the sea?

Her mouth worked soundlessly but couldn't form a single word.

"It will be alright." Belen cleared her throat and drew herself up taller. "Now, is there anything I can get for you? Dry clothes perhaps?" She motioned to Reva's dripping dress.

"Well, I was hoping I'd be allowed to go home, actually." She drummed her fingers against her thighs. "But I'm guessing I'll be stuck here for a while, won't I?"

Belen winced and reached out to take her hand again, linking Reva's arm through her own and turning her in the same direction Jareth had gone. "Yes, for a little while at least. I'm sure…I'm sure Jareth has a plan to get you home as quickly as possible. For now—dry clothes. And perhaps a room. Are you tired?"

Reva murmured a non-committal answer. Truthfully, she felt weary to the bone, but her thoughts raged tumultuously and would probably keep her awake even if her body needed rest.

The grotto wound past half a dozen more "windows" to the ocean beyond. She saw not only jellyfish but a wide variety of other glowing creatures—fish, eels, kraken, and other creatures she simply had no words to describe. As they walked, a steady stream of warmth seemed to seep between Belen's skin and her own.

The tunnel opened into a wider antechamber filled with cupboards and chests of all sizes. Belen stopped at a wardrobe to retrieve a cloak of midnight blue. She slung it around Reva's shoulders and clasped it with a seashell pin just below her throat.

"Um, thank you," Reva said, uncomfortable with the attention. At home, while she was treated with deferential treatment, her people knew she preferred to be treated like one of them and didn't fuss over her unless she asked for help.

They followed another tunnel, and another, until they stepped onto a wide street leading into a huge chamber. Reva's head tipped back in awe as she stared at the columns rising all around her to support an invisible ceiling high above her head. A school of neon-pink fish darted by just outside the invisible barrier.

Belen led her down a street populated by half a dozen Argosan citizens. They gave the two princesses flanked by the guards a wide berth. Reva's boots squeaked against the smooth stone floor as they crossed the courtyard.

At the far side, Reva skidded to an abrupt halt. A wall of sheer sea glass rose to her left, as tall as a three-story building. Through its wavy panes, she caught her first glimpse of Argos. Schools of fish darted around the other chambers carved from rock. Light spilled from windows and illuminated kelp wafting in the ocean currents through the inky black water. Turrets rose all around the seabed beyond the glass wall, guarded by elves astride glowing krakens, their brilliant hues ranging from soft pink to brilliant red.

"I never imagined the bottom of the ocean would be so beautiful," Reva said as Belen joined her at the glass wall.

The elvish princess smiled. "It's beautiful, isn't it? I think you're the first human to ever see Argos. And—" Her voice dropped a few pitches. "—you'll probably be the last, I fear."

Reva's stomach knotted, her awe now tinged with guilt. But it wasn't her fault Argos was in danger. Something moved at the far side of the seabed, beyond the kraken guards and watchtowers. Reva pressed her nose close to the glass and squinted. Something massive seemed to be stirring the waters just beyond the glow from the farthest tower…

"Is that…"

"Calypso," Belen said as she splayed her palm against the glass. "The oldest kraken in the ocean. The last of the greats."

"The one who's dying," Reva said as the water continued to stir in the darkness. She thought she caught the flash of a pale sucker, so large it must have been the size of a building. If the suckers on the kraken's arms were that big…. Her tongue stuck to the roof of her mouth as she tried to imagine how big this creature must really be.

It was bigger than an entire city. Perhaps bigger than an island kingdom.

The ocean outside the glass seemed to press against it, closing in on her, making her feel small and vulnerable.

"Come on." Belen tugged at her arm. "I want you to meet our little sister. She's painting in the gallery in the next bubble."

"Bubble?" Reva tore herself away from the glass wall with reluctance.

"That's what we call the different chambers in Argos. They're all connected by tunnels and grottos, but the main chambers we call bubbles."

The gallery lay just beyond a wide, windowless passage, with thousands of gilded frames stretched in front of them. Reva had never seen so many paintings in her life—her tiny island kingdom had nothing of this magnitude to offer. At the far end of the chamber, a thin girl with short, raven-black hair sat before an easel. She held a plate in one hand smeared with globs of paint. In the other, she held a brush that she swept against a canvas.

"Ophelia, I'd like you to meet a guest," Belen said as they approached.

The girl on the stool did not respond but continued with her work. Reva peered over her shoulder at the ocean landscape recreated by the girl's painting. She'd never seen anything so realistically rendered. As she stared at the painting, she had the sensation she could walk right into it and swim away.

"Ophelia?" Belen repeated.

Still, the girl did not answer. That's when Reva noticed that the elf girl's eyes were not even open.

Ophelia painted with her eyelids shut, an expression of contentment on her face. Belen reached out and took the brush from the young girl's hand. Only then did Ophelia turn to greet them. She glanced over them with only idle interest, her gaze unfocused and lost.

"Ophelia," Belen said once again, with gentle patience, using her free hand to wipe away a glob of blue paint half-dried into Ophelia's chin length hair. "This is Reva. She is the human princess Jareth told you about. Do you remember?"

Ophelia frowned at Belen without once acknowledging Reva. "No," she said curtly as she reclaimed her brush and turned back to the canvas. "Go away."

Reva wasn't sure if she should laugh or feel insulted. Belen shot her an apologetic look and motioned for Reva to walk back toward the main corridor. "I'm sorry," Belen said as they left the gallery behind. "Ophelia is special. She doesn't exactly see the world the way the rest of us do. She's sweet when you can pull her away from her paintbrushes."

The guard to Reva's left coughed quietly.

Belen laughed out loud, the unexpected sound echoing off the tunnel walls. "All right." She shot an amused look over her shoulder before leading them down the tunnel to another turnoff. "I confess she can be irrationally *grumpy* when you interrupt her painting. She was exercising restraint today, to be honest."

They entered another courtyard, this one much noisier than the last. Small elvish children darted around potted plants and vendors dragging small carts loaded with goods. An old elvish lady wearing a shawl that looked to be made of woven seaweed chanted about delectable sweet rolls that couldn't be found anywhere else in Argos. Across the path from her, another elderly vendor barked back that *her* rolls were the best to be had.

They wove between the clusters of shouting children until Belen paused beside a large sandpit where children of all ages appeared to be practicing athletics. They spun and jumped and tossed one another high into the air. One girl who appeared to be around fourteen-year-old landed in a crouch close to them, wearing nothing more than a sleeveless tunic and knee-length britches. The girl's black hair was pulled back in two messy knots on top of her head.

Reva eyed her ensemble with no small amount of envy. Cassandra would have a cow if Reva ever tried to wear something like this outside of her bedchamber…however, it looked excessively practical for physical activity.

Then, the girl tossed her head back with a laugh and bounced to her feet, waving at Belen.

"Did you see that?" She jogged toward them, dodging around her companions to reach the edge of the sandpit. "I *smashed* that landing."

Belen laughed as the girl stopped in front of them, bouncing up and down on her toes. "Yes, I saw. Stop jiggling for a moment, will you? I want you to meet someone."

The girl rolled her eyes but planted her feet firmly in the sand, hands on her bony hips, and looked impatiently at Reva. After only a moment, however, her piercing blue eyes widened. "Wait. Is this her? She's the human, isn't she?"

"Princess Reva Morrigan," Belen said, motioning first to Reva and then to the young girl, "meet my youngest sister, Damaris. Watch out for this one: she bites."

Damaris clacked her teeth and flashed a savage smile at Reva. "Don't listen to her: I'm an angel."

"With horns and a tail," Belen muttered under her breath.

Damaris and Reva laughed in unison. The angel princess hooted and performed a perfectly poised backflip, kicking sand into the air around her. She landed with a thump and threw her arms high in a gesture of triumph.

Reva loved her instantly, this wild child who didn't hide herself behind downcast eyes and meekly folded hands. She saw herself as she was three years ago—a girl with no father or mother, only a stepmother she didn't like and a kingdom waiting for her to grow up and become the queen they needed her to be.

A girl who wasn't afraid of bloody knees and bruised knuckles.

A girl who would rather walk the decks of ships than read about them.

She clapped her hands in approval and couldn't restrain the raw admiration and kinship she already felt for this elf girl. "I think you and I will be wonderful friends."

Damaris grinned back. Then she pursed her lips and swept a critical gaze over Reva. "What do you like? Acrobatics? Knife throwing? Bow and arrows?"

"Damaris," Belen said around a groan.

"Swords." Reva didn't even have to think about it. "I'm also not half bad with the knife throwing, but my aim could use improvement."

Damaris's eyes gleamed. "Oh, I *do* like you." She turned to the side and cupped her hands over her mouth, bellowing: "Charis, bring me some swords!"

"Absolutely not!" Belen grabbed Reva by the arm and tugged her away from the sandpit. "Jareth would murder me. You two can compare your swords later."

Swallowing her disappointment, Reva cast Damaris an apologetic look over her shoulder. But Damaris just grinned and waved merrily before diving back into the jumping, tumbling throng of elf children.

"I like her," Reva said as Belen ushered her across the courtyard.

Belen laughed and rolled her eyes. "Jareth does too. I can see why he chose you."

The warmth drained from Reva's body, overshadowed by the ever-present anxiety. Perhaps Belen had meant her words to be complimentary, but they felt more like barbs.

Had there ever been any *choice*?

Jareth had clearly chosen the only eligible princess on the market—and he'd tried to seal her fate with a kiss she hadn't asked for. Then, instead of freeing her from the *Andromeda,* he'd dragged her to a new prison.

"Ah, here we are." Belen's soothing voice dragged her back to the present. They'd entered a small grotto lit by several orbs, filled with fish, that hung from the ceiling. "There are clothes in the wardrobe. Help yourself to anything you find. If you're tired, I can let you rest—or I can bring you something to eat?"

"I'd like to see Jareth, please," Reva said without hesitation.

Belen's smile faltered, and her posture stiffened as she turned from the wardrobe she'd begun to open. "I think he needs some time—"

"Time is something neither of us have." When Belen flinched, Reva did as well. "I'm sorry to be harsh, but your brother brought this on himself. He brought me here, and now he must deal with me. Please, find him and inform him that I will be expecting an audience in half an hour."

Belen hesitated but then turned to retrieve something from the wardrobe. She padded across the twisted seaweed rug and held out a blanket. "You can use this to dry off," she said quietly. "I'll go find Jareth."

"Thank you." Reva accepted the thick blanket, burying her chilled fingers in the fabric. While a little rough to the touch, it warmed her skin.

Belen dipped her chin and slipped past Reva toward the door. She hesitated, however, and turned back, one hand on the seashell handle. "If I may, Your Highness," she said, pausing to purse her lips. "I know what my brother did is unforgivable. But try to remember—your kingdom isn't the only one at risk. Please. That's all I ask."

Reva flinched, the faces of Ophelia the artist and Damaris the wild girl flashing through her thoughts. The door closed and left her alone, yet she felt haunted by the faces of girls…girls whose lives hung in the balance.

Calix squeaked in her pocket. She tucked the blanket under one arm and fished him out with her free hand. He purred and wrapped his tentacles around her fingers, blinking bulbous eyes as she held him level with her face.

"What am I going to do, Calix?" she whispered. A tear leaked from her eye and ran down her cheek. "There just isn't enough of me to go around."

The kraken reached out a tiny arm and pressed it against the tear at the edge of her jaw. But another tear escaped and trailed after the first. It ran over his pink tentacle before dripping to the polished sea-stone floor.

Reva drew a shuddering breath. "I can't shake the awful feeling, Calix, that no matter what I decide to do…people are going to die."

CHAPTER FOURTEEN

Reva shivered and wrinkled her nose against the dank smell of old socks as Belen escorted her down a waterlogged, dripping tunnel. She wished she had brought the blanket with her as a chill rippled over her skin. The midnight blue dress she'd chosen from the wardrobe didn't have any sleeves and draped from one shoulder, leaving the other completely bare.

She'd picked it because she knew the scandalous off-shoulder design would have appalled Cassandra. Considering current circumstances, she wasn't keen on earning her stepmother's approval or staying in her good graces…

But that was a battle to be fought later.

"I'm sorry about this," Belen said.

Something crunched unpleasantly beneath the heel of the flimsy sandals she'd also borrowed from the cupboard. She'd better start preparing herself for the more immediate battle on her horizon. "Sorry about what?" She hated how the straps on her new footwear wound up over her ankles without offering any real support at all.

Perfectly useless things.

With her dress hiked about her knees to keep it off the wet floor, Belen stalked around a bend in the tunnel as if she hadn't heard Reva's question. "He insisted. He says he knows best. He says you need to see this. Well, I say he's a love-besotted fool. And a half-brained one, at that."

Belen skidded to a halt before a closed door flanked by two elvish guards. They dipped their heads to the princess before casting curious looks at Reva. "I don't suppose the anteroom has flooded and swept my fool brother out into the cold, has it?"

The taller of the two guards scratched behind his ear with the hand not holding his trident. "Ah, no, my lady. Rest assured, it hasn't."

"Pity. Oh well." She turned back to Reva and studied her with a critical eye. "You'll have to talk sense into him then, I suppose. But be quick about it—this bubble is unstable. You look lovely, by the way. That color will drive him crazy."

Reva stiffened, her knuckles whitening around the wad of midnight blue fabric she held off the floor. "Why is that?"

Belen's chilly fingers brushed Reva's collarbone as she adjusted the starfish clasp on the borrowed dress. "My mother had blue eyes," she said matter-of-factly. "I don't remember her well: she returned to the sea when Damaris was born, and I was such a little waif, I only remember taking care of the new baby. But Jareth remembers."

"Returned to the sea?" Reva asked, allowing Belen to finish adjusting the shoulder of the dress.

Belen tipped her head back to look Reva in the face. "She died," she said without a quaver to her voice. "It's our way, to return them to the sea."

Reva flinched and fought hard not to look away. "I see. I'm sorry. My—my father also returned to the sea. He spent as much time on the *Perseus* as he did on land, so we gave him a sailor's burial."

Belen smiled then, but this time emotion twisted her lips in a sad and wistful way. "Well, we might as well be sisters. But I'll leave that to my brother to sort out. Off you go then."

One of the guards opened the door for Reva and stepped aside to let her enter alone. She grimaced and eased into the chamber beyond, a long narrow corridor lit by only a single fish lamp at the far end. Gloom and a headier smell of mildew greeted her as she strode toward the shadowy figure at the end of the tunnel and braced herself for whatever Jareth had planned.

He didn't look at her as she approached but stood with hands locked at the small of his back, staring through one of the strange paneless windows. The invisible barrier stretched from floor to ceiling and gave her a disconcerting view of the shadowy ocean beyond. As she came alongside Jareth, however, she realized she wasn't looking at the ocean but another chamber.

Except it was underwater.

Two elves swam in the chamber beyond, lighting their way with fish lamps strapped to the armor encasing their chests.

"This is the chamber that flooded this morning," she guessed quietly, stopping beside Jareth.

It made sense now why he wanted her to see this. Perhaps he hoped to shock or guilt her into helping him.

Jareth exhaled slowly but didn't tear his attention away from the work beyond the barrier. "It is. They're salvaging what can be saved."

"I'm sorry."

"I should have been here." His whispered confession hinted at a suffering she didn't understand but could imagine.

She also was not where she was meant to be.

"I know I shouldn't have brought you here," he said, lifting a hand to press his palm against the barrier. "But I needed you to see this. I wanted you to understand that this is my heart. This city. This place. These people. I would do anything for them, Reva."

Reva felt a tugging at her heartstrings. The earnest declaration resonated with her, as if he were speaking the words of her own heart. In the end, was that not why she'd been at Black Rock? Why she was still trying to work out an arrangement with Felix? To preserve her people, her kingdom?

She drew a bracing breath. "Jareth, I understand what you're trying to tell me. I do. And I can't deny that I feel something for you and your people. However—"

The hope that flared briefly in his gaze transformed to panic. "No. Please don't."

"*However,*" she repeated as firmly as she could, even though her heart whispered this couldn't be the right choice. "I cannot simply abandon my duties to my own people. Jareth. My people are starving. And if I don't find a solution, I'll lose my people too."

"But I told you that we'd help find food solutions. We just need a safe place to go. I'm not asking you to feed my people. I'll worry about that. And I promise to help you figure out a way to feed your people too. It may take some time, but I know our people can coexist."

She hesitated. "And that right there is the problem, Jareth. Neither of us have *time* to figure this out. My people are starving *now.* We're at the end of the growing season: many of my people won't last until spring let alone until the next harvest."

"And Calypso is dying as we speak! We lost three people today, Reva. Three innocent people who shouldn't have returned to the sea yet. But they're gone."

Jareth grabbed her hand and pressed it against the invisible barrier, pinning it in place. Reva tried to tug it free, but she couldn't help staring into the chamber beyond. A chamber that had returned to the sea and taken lives with it. Tears pricked her eyes.

Reva refused to look at him and made herself stare into the gloom beyond the barrier, at the sea elves salvaging supplies from the wreckage. "You need to take me home, Jareth," she whispered.

"I can't." He caught her by the shoulders and turned her to face him. "Because I'll be taking you home and giving you to *him.* He doesn't love you, Reva, and he doesn't care for your people. He barely cares for his own people. He's using you."

The horrors she'd witnessed at Black Rock flooded over her memories in pulsing waves. "And how are you any better?" She stared at his mouth, refusing to look him in the eye.

She wasn't sure she could stay strong if she faced him.

Jareth's hands tightened around her exposed arms. "I'm not." He barely breathed the words, and she felt the warmth of his breath against her cheeks.

Reva let her gaze slide past his nose to the eyes that stared at her. What had Belen said? That he looked at her like he was drowning? The tears she'd been holding back pressed more fiercely against her eyes. She inhaled raggedly and tried to swallow them back.

"I'm just as bad as Felix," he said.

Was that sheen in his eyes a trick of the fish lamp?

"I went to Black Rock because I needed you to help me save my people."

"Jareth," she choked. "*I can't.* I'm just one person, and I don't have the magic of the sea behind me. You're asking too much!"

"But when I saw you standing on that beach, Reva." He ignored her arguments and tugged her closer. "When you jumped into that boat and rowed out to sea to save Felix's people…"

She closed her eyes against an onslaught of images—burning timbers, floating bodies, bloody wounds…

"I didn't see a princess," he said.

Her eyes flew open, searching for the meaning behind his words.

"I didn't see a princess," he repeated. "I saw a queen who would do anything to save the innocent. I saw a queen who was as at home on the sea as she was on the land. A queen who wasn't afraid to walk in two worlds. Who wasn't afraid of risk and danger. And I knew. I *knew* in that moment that—that—"

As his voice broke, a tear escaped at last and trailed down her cheek. This tear fell along and unhindered, because little Calix was hiding in her pocket and wasn't there to catch it.

"You knew what?" she asked, unable to squelch her own foolish curiosity.

"I knew that there wasn't any other woman for me. Only you. And if you couldn't save me, no one ever would."

She squeezed her eyes closed against the thinly veiled confession in his words. "What are you trying to say, Jareth?"

"I love you, Reva, as crazy as that sounds. I've loved you since I first saw you in that blasted dinghy with the sun on your skin, and the wind and salt in your hair, and determination in your heart—"

"Please, don't."

"I have to. Because if I don't speak now, I'll lose you forever. I'll never have another opportunity. This is my one and only chance, Reva."

Reva forced her eyes open. She owed him that much—to look him in the eye when she broke his heart. "I don't know what to say to that," she said gently. "I don't know where I begin and where your magic ends. You've got me so twisted up, Jareth. What you're asking…it isn't fair."

"No. It's not."

"And if I were the sort of princess who stood on the beach and let others fight her battles for her…perhaps my answer would be different. But I'm not. You know that as well as I do. What I want can't factor into this. If I was free to choose what my heart wanted instead of what duty demanded…perhaps things would be different. But I'm not that kind of princess. You need to let me go."

Jareth turned his face away and slid his fingers down her arms before withdrawing and leaving her aching and chilled. Once again, he was only doing what she'd asked him to do, so why did it feel so wrong?

"I will do what I can for your people, Jareth. I can at least offer temporary sanctuary for the elderly and little ones who are most in danger. But beyond that…"

It had sounded like a good plan when she thought it, but as she formed the words, a new sort of pain stabbed at her heart.

She was going to walk away from this *and marry* Felix. *Had she lost her mind?*

Because, in spite of everything he'd done, she couldn't shake the feeling that if anyone were to stand beside her on the day of her coronation…she'd want it to be Jareth.

Not Felix. Not Rency. Just Jareth.

Someone who would fight beside her to save people…not watch as they died alone.

"This is the only way to ensure the safety of my people. I can't risk war on top of food shortages…" she said out loud, for herself, for him. "What I want can't matter."

Jareth's face snapped toward her again, and he swayed as if he might reach for her again. But he didn't.

She doubted Felix would ever show such restraint or respect for her wishes.

Reva steeled her spine and squared her shoulders. She searched inside herself for that feral queen Jareth said he saw inside her, the one she wore as a mask to hide the fragile girl she really was.

But this time, it couldn't be just a mask. She needed to be that queen.

"Please." Jareth searched her face as if she were the last gasp of air in Rhuin. "I-I want to kiss you so badly right now."

Heat warmed her cheeks as her heart thundered against her rib cage. "You've already kissed me twice," she reminded him hoarsely. Were these emotions even hers?

Or were they the result of his siren kiss?

He inched closer, his fingers twitching at his sides. "Is that permission?" A flicker of hope gleamed in Jareth's sea-green eyes.

And for one desperate moment Reva almost said yes. It would be so easy to pretend, even for just a moment, that nothing else mattered. That she was a girl, and he was a boy, and there weren't any kingdoms between them.

But that wasn't fair to him, and she'd never been one to embrace fairy tales.

"Take me home, Jareth," she said around the suffocating lump in her throat. "And—and please don't kiss me ever again."

Jareth recoiled, squeezing his eyes closed as he half-turned away from her. She could see his fingers clenching and releasing at his sides in frantic motion, and she'd never hated herself more than she did in that moment.

She couldn't watch this anymore. Spinning on her heel, Reva pressed a fist against her mouth and stumbled toward the door, her sandals slapping against the stone floor.

This was the right thing to do…to sacrifice her own happiness for her people… Then why did it feel like it wasn't only his heart she'd broken but also her own?

Belen and the guards still waited for her beyond the door. The elf princess took a step toward Reva but faltered as she took in Reva's twisted expression. Hopelessness stole over Belen's delicate features, and she drew herself up as tall as her small stature would allow.

"I see," she said quietly. "The decision's been made then."

"Please," Reva choked, wishing she could explain. "Make him take me home now, please."

After a stilted meal in the guest room, Belen found Reva more practical clothes for the journey home. Dressed in knee britches and a loose-fitting tunic that cinched at the waist with a scarlet sash, Reva slipped into the long coat Belen had also provided. Her boots still squished, soaked with water, but she forced her feet into them.

Calix sat on the bed, squeaking and waving his limbs in agitation. She scooped him up and patted him on the top of his round head. "You're going to have to go back to Jareth, you know," she said as he squelched up her arm and tried to reach for her coat pocket. She shifted to allow him access and smiled as he dove into the pocket with a happy chirp.

Belen and her entourage of guards were silent as they led Reva through Argos, back to the chamber where she'd first arrived. She couldn't help but imagine their disappointment and disapproval.

But the decision and risks were hers alone to take.

Jareth was waiting when they arrived, expressionless. Belen reached up to touch his cheek before turning to Reva to say her goodbyes.

"It was wonderful to meet you," she said sincerely. "I do wish you the best. Hopefully we'll meet again one day."

Reva nodded but couldn't speak past the lump in her throat. She watched in silence as Belen and her guards exited the grotto, leaving her alone with Jareth once more. They stared at one another without speaking until Reva worked up the nerve to move closer.

She wasn't looking forward to what came next.

Jareth inhaled a ragged breath—apparently, he wasn't either. "I can't do this without—without—"

Reva winced, already aware of the direction his thoughts had wandered. "You may breathe for me, Jareth." Her voice quavered, but she lifted her chin and demanded calm from herself. "Just breathing."

He offered a curt nod and reached for her hand to draw her closer. She shivered and took deep, stabilizing breaths.

"I'm sorry there isn't another way," he said.

"I'll be fine. At least I know what to expect now. I'm getting quite good at this kissing and not drowning thing."

Something flickered in Jareth's gaze, and Reva wondered if she shouldn't have mentioned the word *kissing*. But it was too late now to rethink her word choice.

Half-laughing to mask her discomfort, Reva let him guide her to the barrier and place her back against it. The coldness of the ocean seeped through the invisible wall. Uncertainty roiled in her belly as Jareth positioned himself squarely in front of her. Why did he have to look as nervous as she felt?

"So, um, how do we get…out?" she asked as he slid his arms around her.

Jareth's arms tightened around the small of her back as he leaned his face toward hers. "Like this," he whispered. Then he barked, "Apollos!"

And he sealed his mouth over hers as kraken arms exploded through the barrier, coiled around them, and dragged them out into the dark sea.

CHAPTER FIFTEEN

Reva's chest ached as she rolled onto her stomach on the foggy beach and tried to inhale. She had thought she'd be more prepared this time, but her lungs still refused to draw in the oxygen they so desperately needed. Jareth crouched beside her, one hand on her shoulder as she struggled.

His touch should have been comforting, but it only made her pain greater. She dug her fingers into the sand and screamed inwardly—not about the agony in her lungs but the ache in her heart.

While she thought she'd been ready for the long journey through the ocean, she hadn't been prepared for the feeling of resting in Jareth's arms. It had been a strange, exhilarating sort of torture, now that she knew how he felt about her…

Why did she have to be strong? Why couldn't she just let herself melt in his arms and forget the rest of the world? Her cheeks burned as she finally managed a small breath.

And now she had to walk away.

As Reva resumed breathing on her own, Jareth withdrew and let her recover alone. She had no one to blame for any of this but herself.

Pulling herself together, Reva stumbled to her feet and tried to brush damp sand from her fingers and clothes, but it clung stubbornly. Calix squirmed in her pocket when she brushed too hard against the side of her trousers.

Muttering an apology, she fished him out and patted his head. Mist hovered above the water, so thick she could only see a few yards behind her. Above her, she could see only one turret of the castle piercing the thick fog, its stones pockmarked from exposure to the elements.

Voices and clamoring reverberated from somewhere inside the castle.

"They're up early," Jareth said quietly as he joined her on the beach. "It's not much past dawn, I'd wager. It took us half the night to get here."

Calix curled his limbs around her fingers and began to purr. A sensation of unease rose in Reva's stomach as she listened to the sounds falling from above them.

"They're up *too* early." When her voice cracked, she thumped a fist against her chest and coughed. "Something's going on."

"I'm sure they're looking for you."

She winced and nodded. This would be a good time to say some sort of farewell, but no words seemed adequate. Calix squeaked as she held him toward Jareth.

"You best take him," she said, unable to conceal the hitch in her voice. "I need to let my people know I'm home."

Jareth's eyebrows lowered, but he reached for Calix. The kraken shrieked and clung more tightly to her fingers, his suckers making loud *pops* as Jareth tried to pry him loose. Reva nearly changed her mind, listening to the tiny creature's wails of distress. She'd gotten so used to him napping in her pocket, like a little fur-less kitten she could take anywhere…

No wonder Jareth's pockets were always full.

But Jareth finally succeeded in sliding his hand across the top of hers to dislodge the baby. Calix continued to writhe and cry as Jareth slipped him into one of his own deep pockets. Only then did the man meet her gaze.

"Should I escort you to the castle?" he asked, stuffing Calix back into his pocket when the little blob managed to escape. Grimacing, Jareth secured the buckle and trapped the poor thing inside his vest.

Calix's frustrated squeaking made Reva feel even worse.

"No, I think it would be best if we said goodbye here," she said uneasily. "It's a safe bet you won't be welcome, and it may take me a while to explain things."

Jareth flinched. "Will I see you again?"

I hope so, she thought, but her lips formed the words, "I don't know," instead. She cleared her throat and forged ahead. "I'm going to try to make arrangements for the children and elderly to come here temporarily. If you can give me a few days to figure out the details—"

"Reva."

She stared down at her boots sinking into the white sand.

"Don't do this." Jareth's hand twitched at his side, and she wondered if he would reach for her, but he didn't. "Don't—don't marry Felix. Please. Is there anything I can say that will change your mind?"

There were a million things he could probably say, but she knew if she gave him an inch of encouragement, she'd never be able to stick to her plan. *Marry Felix. Feed your people.*

"I'm sorry, Jareth," she finally managed.

Then she spun on her heel and dashed across the sand, away from the sea, away from him.

Why did it feel as if an invisible cord were pulling her back? And why did she still feel like she was making a terrible mistake?

When Reva reached the stone staircase that would take her from the beach to the top of the first ring of cliffs, she nearly succumbed to the desire to look back. Faltering on the bottom step, she gripped the stone railing and gathered the last of her determination.

This was best for her people, and she *needed* to stay strong, no matter what it cost her personally.

And so she climbed.

The din inside the castle grew louder the higher she ran. Instead of taking the fork in the staircase that would lead to the main courtyard, Reva took the narrower path that climbed around the outside of the cliffs. It would lead her around to a side entrance that overlooked the western sea. It shouldn't be as busy, and she'd be able to slip inside without having to explain to a dozen people how she had managed to get home on her own.

She hoped anyway.

Reva left the exterior staircase when it opened onto a small rock outcropping that served as a balcony. The castle warmth wrapped around her when she slipped through the back door, entering the narrow hallway that led to the servants' stairway.

Loud voices clamored from the lower levels. Reva hesitated before turning and running up the staircase instead of down to the servant passages. She'd enter the backside of the guest wing, in the hidden servant stairs, slip through one of the rooms, and then enter the main hall that led to the royal family suites. Hopefully she would find Cassandra still in her morning toilette.

She didn't want an audience when she faced her stepmother. Things were going to be said…and they wouldn't be pleasant.

A faint thumping noise echoed down the stone staircase as Reva trotted higher into the castle. It grew to an incessant banging, interspersed with muffled yells. She hesitated at the end of the hallway and focused, trying to pinpoint where the sound was coming from.

It only took her a moment to discover the banging came from inside the third guest room from the end of the wing.

The servant's entrance had been bolted from the *outside*. A wooden plank ran across the doorway, held in place by two makeshift brackets. It wasn't uncommon for guests to bolt the door from the inside when they didn't want to be disturbed. But why had the servants barred the door from without?

The door shook with renewed banging.

"*Let me out!*" came the muffled bellow from within.

"Who's in there?" she called back.

"*I am Prince Felix, third son and heir to His Royal Majesty—*"

Reva unbolted the door and yanked it open, allowing the third son and royal heir to spill into the hallway. He staggered and gripped the doorframe to catch his balance. The sunburn on his nose was further complimented by the fiery red blush staining his cheeks.

"You!" He jabbed a finger at her. "You're back!"

She resisted the urge to slap away his finger. "I am. Why are you locked in a guestroom? What did you do?"

"What did *I* do?" His face deepened to an even more unsightly shade of red. "I didn't do a blasted thing. It's your stepmother. She's gone completely mad!"

Reva shushed him by waving both hands. "Lower your voice and tell me what's happened. Calmly."

He inhaled a ragged breath and leaned against the doorframe, mopping his forehead with the sleeve of his wrinkled tunic. "Your stepmother has taken leave of her senses!"

"So you've said. Why did she lock you up, Felix?"

Felix's eyes narrowed, and he leaned toward Reva, lowering his voice to barely more than a whisper. "Because I told her I wouldn't go along with her dirty scheme any longer, that's why."

Reva's jaw tightened, her pulse thundering against her temples. "Pray tell," she began in a deadly calm whisper, "what dirty scheme is this? The one where you force me into marriage so that she can steal my kingdom? Or the other one where you plan to have me assassinated?"

He'd already begun to forge ahead but faltered into silence as her words actually penetrated his deaf ears. "Don't look so angry," he said, uneasily flicking away a bit of lint on the front of his shirt. "None of that was my idea. We both know she's a conniving old hag, the way she's been trying to force me to marry you."

Reva pursed her lips and wondered if she could believe anything he said. "So you want me to believe the marriage scheme wasn't your plan?"

Felix shot her a withering look. "You don't think I wanted to marry *you*, did you? No, Cassandra found out that I've been—that I may have—never mind, she found out something I'd rather my father not know, and she threatened to expose me if I didn't do what she wanted."

"What did she find out?"

"That's none of your business—"

She grabbed the handle of the door and began to swing it toward him. He caught it with one hand and wedged himself in the doorway. "No, no! Wait! I've been siphoning money from the royal coffers, and somehow her spies found out about it. It's for purely selfless reasons, I can assure you—"

Somehow, none of this surprised her *or* seemed unbelievable. Why would he make up such a horrendous lie? "You're a petty thief. Just like Rency."

His eyes narrowed. "I am *not*. I can't believe you'd compare me to a pirate."

"But you've been stealing from your own father!" Reva leaned her weight into the door, but the prince of Desta wouldn't budge.

"Because I'm trying to save the woman I *actually* want to marry from slavery, that's why! When my father found out about me and Felicity, he sold her to the mainland as an indentured servant."

Reva eased her weight off the door, staring at the prince. "You're trying to tell me that your father actually sold your lady fair into slavery because he didn't want you to marry her?"

"He did." When Felix pushed against the door, she eased back and let him. "He has higher aspirations for me, but I want Felicity. I don't care if she's a commoner. I'm going to marry her, and I'll steal every penny out from under his nose if that's what it takes to free her."

Reva squeezed the bridge of her nose. This was the most ludicrous tale she'd ever heard, but somehow she didn't think Felix possessed enough creativity in him to make it up. "And when you told Cassandra you'd changed your mind about marrying *me,* she locked you up?"

"Well, no, not exactly. When I told her I was going to have her hanged for blowing up the *Endellion,* that's when she locked me up."

Reva exhaled slowly to mask a small shard of disappointment, of pain. A part of her had still been clinging to the hope that Cassandra really wasn't to blame for any of this…that she *hadn't* been scheming all these years.

Smiling in Reva's face when she planned all along to stab her in the back.

Felix ran his fingers through his disheveled hair. "When you disappeared, I suspected Cassandra had taken things too far, and when I went to confront her, I caught her using a Death Pearl, and—"

"Wait!"

"—and while I may not be kingly material, I paid attention in my history lessons, and I know dark magic when I see it. Don't ask me where she got a Death Pearl, but she's using it, I tell you. She blew up my ship, and she's the one who tried to have you assassinated—and why are you flapping your hands at me?"

"Because you won't shut up!" Reva clapped her hands over his mouth and glared at him. "I'm going to deal with Cassandra, have no doubts about that. But I'm going to need your help, and if you'll stop talking long enough to listen, I think we can find an arrangement that will be beneficial to both of us."

Felix's pale eyes narrowed. When his lips parted beneath the palm of her hand, she pressed harder against his mouth until he nodded in submission.

"Now listen," she ordered, pulling her hand away and wiping it on her trousers. "How much money have you stolen from your father? Do you have access to it?"

"Enough to set Felicity up like the princess she should be," Felix said with a smirk. "My father always underestimated me—"

He broke off when Reva took a menacing step toward him again.

"That's good," she said. "So, here's my proposal. If I rescue Felicity and offer you a place to live in Etthan—

outside your father's hold—will you give me the money you've stolen to buy food for my people?"

"No. That money is to rescue *Felicity*—"

"I'm not planning to buy her freedom. We're going to *steal* her back—don't look so shocked. You're clearly good at that. And after you get her back, I'll make sure you both have everything you need. But either you give me the money to feed my people, or you're going to have to marry me so your father gets his trade routes."

"And how do you expect to find her?"

Reva exhaled and braced herself for the fight she knew would be coming. "I know a man who'll be perfect for this assignment."

"Rency." Felix's eyes narrowed and his voice took on a dangerous edge. "So you get food, and I get Felicity, but what does Rency get out of this hypothetical arrangement?"

"Not being hung," Reva answered. "That's what he gets."

"He's a pirate—he'll come up with a third option that doesn't benefit either of us."

Reva frowned. "He'll probably try, but we'll just have to make sure he doesn't get a chance to do that, won't we?"

Felix's eyes glinted with ill humor, but he finally heaved an exasperated sigh. "Well, I don't see what choice I have. Cassandra has me backed into a corner, and unless we deal with *her*, I won't have any money to give you *or* Felicity."

"Then let's go deal with her. You and me." She arched one eyebrow and waited for him to make his decision.

"How do I know I can trust you?" Felix crossed his arms over his chest and studied the floor. While the words were petulant, a muscle twitched his jaw. That—combined with the tense set of his shoulders—suggested to Reva that he really was worried about this girl of his.

"Do I look like I want to marry *you?*" she asked, echoing his words from earlier. "Unless we want to get stuck in this arrangement, we have no choice but to trust one another."

That muscle twitched in his jaw again, but the prince finally met her gaze. "Very well. But if you don't hold up your end of the bargain and we get stuck with one another, I promise I'll make your life absolutely miserable."

"That goes both ways."

He glared at her but stuck his hand out. "It's a deal then."

Reva hesitated only a moment before she gripped the clammy hand he offered. She released him and stepped back, motioning for him to join her in the servant's corridor. "Now that we've settled that, let's find Cassandra and put an end to this."

Felix stepped into the hall and kicked the door closed behind him; the entire corridor shook from the impact. Reva staggered and shot him a startled look. Somehow, she found it surprising that he had enough strength in his spineless body to deliver such a resounding—

The hallway shook again, as if a shiver had torn through the entire castle.

"What the—"

Outside, alarm bells began clanging.

CHAPTER SIXTEEN

The peals of the alarms echoed through the castle, joined by frantic voices from outside the castle walls. Reva strode to the nearest window and threw open the wooden shutters. Leaning through the window, she strained to see what was wrong.

Outside in the cove, a long, black tentacle rose out of the ocean and reached toward the castle. *No, not again...*

As a second smoky black tentacle rose out of the sea, Felix pressed against Reva for a spot at the window, his pale hand gripping the sill. One of the enormous tentacles swept at the battlement below their window, scattering screaming soldiers in its wake.

Reva jammed a fist against her mouth.

Felix swore. "Is that—is that a kraken?"

"I think it's Cassandra's Death Pearl magic." Horror clawed at the back of Reva's throat as the beast that had torn apart the *Endellion* and tried to sink the *Andromeda* now stretched its horrible arms toward Etthan—toward her home and her people.

"You've seen this before?" Real fear tainted the prince's voice.

Reva nodded, unable to speak. They both flinched as a third tentacle descended on the lower battlements, shaking the castle with a bone-shattering boom. Dust shook free of the ceiling and drifted down on their heads and shoulders.

Felix clutched her wrist. "We need to get out of the castle. Go inland, where it can't reach us—"

Screams from below tore Reva out of her horror and back into her own body. "No!" She wrenched away from Felix. "I'm not going to leave my people to die. Look at that thing—my people will be slaughtered!"

She wanted to clap her hands over her ears, shielding herself from the cries of screaming men falling to their deaths, of wounded soldiers being crushed by the monster's ever-growing black tentacles.

But she would not leave her people to this fate. Not while she had breath in her body. This all came back to Cassandra, to the regent who wanted to be queen so badly she'd make a deal with a monster to get what she wanted. Reva spun, reaching to pull Felix after her—

Only to watch Felix hightailing it toward the servants' staircase as fast as his land-loving legs could take him.

"Felix, you coward!" she bawled.

She hoped Cassandra's kraken smashed him to pulp.

Reva bolted for the nearest guestroom, dashing around the furniture in the dark chamber to reach the door to the main hallway. From there, she dashed toward the family's wing of the palace with only one plan in her mind:

Save Etthan.

If Felix was right, and Cassandra was using dark magic…maybe stopping *her* would stop the monster.

Reaching her stepmother's door, she found it open. Reva halted for a moment to catch her breath—to still her aching, pounding heart—then went inside.

Utter silence greeted her, the room dark, the curtains and adjacent rooms closed off. All except one. The door that led to the balcony lay open a crack, allowing a shaft of light to flood into Cassandra's main room, piercing the gloom.

With a growing sense of dread, Reva forced herself to open the door and walk into the daylight, to ascend the steps and race out onto the stone parapet.

Cassandra stood at the stone railing, dressed in a blood—red gown. She faced the sea and the monstrous shadow kraken which continued to claw its way out of the waves toward the castle.

"Cassandra, what are you doing?" Reva dashed toward her stepmother, but Cassandra didn't answer.

Reva reached to grab her by the arm but faltered when she saw what Cassandra held so tightly in her hands.

A huge black pearl, as large as a man's fist. Wind coiled about Cassandra, tangling her skirts and hair, nearly drowning out the strange, unfamiliar words that fell from her lips.

"Cassandra?" Pain twisted Reva's words into something that sounded weak and lost.

Still, her stepmother didn't acknowledge her but continued to mutter dark words as she stared at the kraken advancing on Etthan. Reva grabbed for the pearl.

This yanked Cassandra out of her stupor. She screamed and jerked away from Reva, clutching the pearl to her chest. "Get out of my way, you stupid girl!"

Reva ignored her and scratched at her stepmother's hands, trying to get her fingers around the pearl. "You need to stop this!"

"I can't stop it!" Cassandra elbowed Reva hard on the chest.

The force of the blow sent her skidding backward, but Reva lurched forward again, more determined than ever to put a stop to this.

"You're going to get everyone killed!" Reva caught hold of Cassandra's arms and clenched as hard as she could, digging her fingernails into the tender flesh on the underside of her stepmother's wrists.

But Cassandra didn't seem to feel anything. Her eyes, wide and crazed and swirling with dark shadows, fixed on Reva with terrifying intensity. "If I stop," she said between gritted teeth, "everyone *will* die."

Reva froze. "What are you talking about?"

"I didn't mean for this to happen," her stepmother said in a tight, pained voice. "The Death Pearl has such power. Such tremendous power. I only meant to use it to call the beast. But after the attack on the *Endellion*, I lost control of the monster. It stopped listening to me."

Reva's pulse throbbed in her temple, but she refused to release her grip on Cassandra. "So you *didn't* send that thing after me?"

"Well…yes." Cassandra twisted her lips into a bitter smile. "You're in the way, Reva—your father should have made me queen, not regent. *Queen!* You're just like your mother, you know. She stole my place first. Your father should have been mine, but he took one look at your mother and fell in love."

Cassandra said the words as if falling in love were a disease that might be catching.

"And then when she died, I thought I might be able to take my place at last. But your weak father willed that *you* become queen on your eighteenth birthday. And what did that make me?"

"A regent, Cassandra. It made you a regent!"

"I don't want to be regent!" Cassandra's scream echoed off the castles of the castle. "I want to be mistress of this gods-forsaken island. I want to throw you into the sea and watch you drown, and I want to kill every last elf in the ocean, and I want—"

"Those things won't make you a queen," Reva said, angry tears burning behind her eyes. "They make you a tyrant. I understand why you may want to get rid of me, but why the elves? What did they ever do to you?"

"They murdered my parents, that's why!" Cassandra's chest rose and fell with frantic breaths. "Before you were born, there was a skirmish between the humans and elves.

My parents went out to battle and never came home. The elves murdered them."

Reva's eyes rolled closed momentarily, as puzzle pieces slowly clicked into place. But Cassandra had twisted everything up so that the truth might never be found. "Cassandra, that was *war*. Terrible things happen in war, but we aren't at war now. Jareth and his sisters aren't the ones who killed your parents—and just like we aren't the ones who went out to fight in that battle. Those were other people, other times. You have to let it go."

"I won't let it go!" Cassandra yanked free of Reva's hold and took a step back. "They ruined my life, made me a sands-blighted orphan. I scraped and fought for every crumb. I gave up everything to earn this crown, *my crown*. And you're not going to take it from me now. Yes, I failed to kill you on that beach, and yes, I failed to sink the *Andromeda*. But I won't fail again."

Anger flared in Reva's belly, but shock held her in its silent grip.

"I'm going to finish what I started. I may have lost control of the kraken, but I can still get what I want. And if you interfere, you're going to get everyone killed. So for once in your life, stand aside and take your proper place on this island. I am Etthan's future. *I am their queen.*"

"You're not a queen," Reva said, tears stinging her eyes as she stared at the woman who should have been guide and protector. "You're a mad woman."

"No," Cassandra said, the unnatural shadows in her eyes coalescing into a single mass that drowned out all hints of color. "I'm Etthan's queen. I'm a queen."

Reva felt bile rise in the back of her throat as she watched this woman succumb to madness.

Then Cassandra screamed a word Reva had never heard. A shockwave drove Reva backward. Her hands slipped off Cassandra, and she skidded across the balcony, slamming into the outside wall of the castle. Stars in her vision mingled with pain in her body.

Groaning, Reva struggled to her feet and took a moment to clear the darkness pressing at her peripherals. Then she advanced on Cassandra again.

"Don't you see?" Cassandra's words were as sharp as a blade. "With every life it takes, that thing gets bigger. It gets *stronger*. And if you interfere, it will become unstoppable. This is the only way."

Another shadowy tentacle smashed against the side of the castle, about fifty yards below them. The impact shook the foundations of the castle. Reva and Cassandra both stumbled. Reva didn't doubt her stepmother was telling the truth—this beast was already five times the size of the one that had attacked the *Andromeda*.

"We need to stop this creature before it destroys Etthan entirely!"

But as Reva drew close to Cassandra again, she realized her stepmother's dark eyes had gone completely black, with madness and magic and who knew what else.

"Too late," Cassandra breathed, in a tone twisted with both fear and fascination. "Too late. With every life it takes, with every drop of blood it spills, it only strengthens."

Fresh screams of terror from below only reinforced how out of control the shadow kraken had become.

"We must do something!" Reva lurched forward and grabbed her stepmother by the shoulders, shaking her. "Jareth can help us. His krakens will help fight the—"

"He can't help you."

"Why not?" Reva clung to Cassandra, digging her fingers into the woman's shoulders.

"Only a blood sacrifice can stop the monster now," Cassandra said as her black eyes stared at Reva, unseeing.

Blood sacrifice.

The words soaked into Reva's thoughts and took root like the blight that had dug into Etthan's soil. Her stomach lurched, and she feared she would vomit all over them both.

What—*or who*—was Cassandra planning to sacrifice?

"What do you mean?" Reva choked the words past clenched teeth and shook her stepmother again. "Tell me!"

Cassandra never answered. She simply lifted her hand and pointed to something above Reva's left shoulder.

Reva released her and spun to search the battlements above them. Her stomach clenched and plummeted when she saw the small crowd gathered on the ledge above them.

"Oh, sand and pearls," she whispered.

Dread slammed her like the kraken's massive, shadowy arms pounding against her castle. Cassandra wasn't planning to stake out a goat to appease the monster. It wasn't *that* sort of blood sacrifice.

It was worse. So much worse.

Above her, on the battlement, half a dozen guards stood around a lone figure stretched between two posts, arms bound and pulled taut.

She would have recognized that elvish form anywhere.

As Cassandra's intentions became clear, Reva's entire body shook with shock. Her stomach tightened into a knot so tight she feared her insides would be crushed.

"This is the only way for me to regain control, Reva," Cassandra said in a tone that held no pity or remorse. "It's either your prince's life…or all of our lives. I've already performed the binding words. There is no other way."

"No," Reva mouthed the word but could manage no sound.

"He must be sacrificed for the good of Etthan. There's no other way."

CHAPTER SEVENTEEN

Something snapped inside Reva, and fury swept her shock to the side. "Have you lost your sand-loving mind?" she screamed at her stepmother. "Murder isn't the answer!"

Cassandra backed away from Reva, still clutching the pearl in both hands. "This is how it must be, Reva. Give up the elf prince. You still have Felix, yes? You can have Felix and his kingdom. I will have Etthan. One little sacrifice, and all that we've dreamed of can be ours."

"Cassandra!" Reva stalked closer to her, fingers curled into fists as a light drizzle began to touch her shoulders.

"This is not *my* dream. Even if I were to marry Felix, his kingdom will never be ours. He's a third son!"

"We have the power now," Cassandra continued as she backed into the railing, as if she hadn't heard anything Reva said. She held up the pearl. "Etthan for me. Desta for you. Together, we will control the routes and waterways. We'll stop the blight. We'll—"

Reva couldn't listen anymore. She drew back a clenched fist and drove it hard toward Cassandra's face. Pain throbbed in her knuckles, and the impact jarred her arm as Cassandra screamed, dropping the pearl and grasping for her injuries. Reva dove for the pearl, scrabbling on the damp stone floor. It finally rolled to a stop, and she snatched up the black orb.

An icy chill ran up her fingertips.

Now if she could only get to Jareth in time—

Hands grabbed her hair and jerked her head back. Shards of pain yanked at her scalp as she stared up at Cassandra's bloodied, feral face.

"You stupid child!" Cassandra flung the words at her so hard, spittle flew from her mouth and mingled with the rainwater splattering against Reva's face.

Reva braced herself for pain and threw her weight backward, into her stepmother's legs. Cursing, Cassandra stumbled to regain her balance. Reva yanked free and rolled to the side, coming up in a low crouch on the slick balcony floor. Her scalp prickled with pain where Cassandra's fingers had torn hair out by the roots.

The castle shook from yet another attack from the kraken. Rock screamed against rock in a cacophony of rending sounds as the south tower *fell*. One minute it stood tall and immobile, and the next it crumpled from the pressure of a coiled arm around its exterior, plummeting in a thousand pieces to the lower levels of the castle.

The floor shuddered beneath her, the stones tumbling in a roar down to the sea.

How many people had been inside that tower?

She didn't have time for this. She needed to get up on the battlement before it was too late, while there was still time to save Jareth and everyone else in Etthan.

Her gaze roamed the distance between her and the battlement, resting on the trellis overrun with vines and crimson sand flowers that stretched from Cassandra's balcony up to the battlement above.

It had held her weight when she was younger…but would it still?

Reva launched toward the trellis, but Cassandra dove for her at the same time, catching Reva around the waist. They skidded sideways and slammed into the wall, Cassandra half sliding through the open doorway as Reva grabbed the door jamb with her free hand. Pain from the jarring impact pulsed through her body. Using the arm that clutched the pearl, she drove her elbow downward, catching Cassandra in the tender hollow where neck met shoulder.

Her stepmother screamed, her arms loosening enough that Reva could tear herself free and race toward the trellis again. She shoved the pearl into the pocket of her trousers and wrapped her hands around trellis and vine. When Cassandra grabbed her by the leg, Reva kicked out with a snarl.

"Let go!" she screamed.

Her boot connected with Cassandra's face, and blood spray mingled with the rain. As Cassandra slumped to the balcony floor, Reva climbed. The trellis shuddered and creaked beneath her weight, but she pressed upward as quickly as she dared, hand over hand. Her boots struggled to find solid footholds, slipping on the winding vines that blocked the trellis boards.

The drizzle turned into a downpour as the sky released its fury on the island below, adding to the madness and confusion of the kraken. Thunder rumbled in the distance, and—in her peripheral vision—Reva glimpsed lightning flashing over the sea. Below her, she heard the screams of her people as a monster born of nightmares spread its arms across the castle.

The kraken's massive, dark form blotted out the gray light of the overcast morning. It was only a matter of time before it would decimate the entire castle. Or before it spotted Jareth, bound on the battlement above Reva, helpless and alone except for the guards—*her guards*—who had staked him out to die.

Because of her.

The trellis shifted beneath Reva's weight. Crying out, she clung tightly to the flimsy structure and tried not to imagine her body plunging to the balcony now far below her. Screams from above pierced through the thunder of rainfall.

She forced her stiff fingers to release and reached for another handhold. Her arms and legs trembled as she neared the top of the trellis, her body aching from the exertion. She paused and studied the distance between her and the thick battlement railing. She'd misjudged the distance.

Several yards of empty wall stretched between her and the battlement.

Reva choked back a cry of frustration and studied the castle wall. Its craggy surface offered potential handholds in the chinks between the stones, but she'd only be able to get the tips of her boots and fingers into them. Bracing herself, Reva reached out a hand and gripped hard before daring to shift her left foot and inch to the side.

Her arms, taut with tension, shook as Reva eased off the trellis and edged her way toward the railing a few feet above her. *Just think about the next handhold,* she thought as she tried not to think about the balcony far below. She shifted her foot across the wall, searching for someplace to dig the toe of her boot into. It scraped across solid wall as she blindly searched for a foothold.

Her stomach tightened as she imagined the inevitable sensation of falling…

A hand grasped her wrist.

Crying out, Reva clung to the wall and tipped her head back to see Rency leaning over the battlement, his blond hair rain-soaked and eyes wide.

"Reva, you fool girl!" he shouted down to her. "What are you doing? Are you trying to get yourself killed? Again?"

She tried to unclench her jaw to answer but couldn't manage it. She dug the fingertips of her other hand into the cracks and kicked her feet as Rency hauled her upward. Her pulse thundered against her skin, every muscle tight and aching. She slid across the thick battlement wall and balanced on her wobbly legs.

Her jaw began to quiver from the strain, from the relief.

Rency allowed her to pull away, but anger darkened his features. "You need to stop trying to kill yourself, because I'm getting tired of trying to save you. It's becoming a thing with us, you know."

"Jareth," she said around chattering teeth.

She darted around the pirate captain and sprinted toward Jareth strung between the pillars at the end of the battlement. Beyond him, the hulking shadow of the kraken rose. The remaining guards screamed and retreated as the creature coiled toward the battlement.

One of the soldiers paused to grab her arm. Behind her, Rency bellowed a, "Get your hands off me, mate!"

"Get out of my way!" she snarled, not caring what they did with Rency as long as it kept him out of her way. "Or you'll feel the full weight of the crown bearing down on you."

The young guard faltered and released her. It wasn't much, but it was enough for her to slip through the scattering line of petrified soldiers and dash toward Jareth. She circled around the pillar on the left.

Jareth lifted his head as she approached, blood oozing from a wound along his hairline, over his forehead, and down his cheek.

"Reva," he whispered as reached up to tug on the ropes that held his arms stretched to the sides.

"I'm here," she said, gasping for air around each word.

"You need to get away."

"Not without you." Reva yanked at the ropes ineffectually. Then she reached into her boot for her knife…but her fingers found an empty sheath where her blade usually rested.

Her eyes closed involuntarily.

"Raging seas, what are you doing?" Jareth's voice rose in the darkness behind her closed eyelids. "Get out of here before you get yourself killed!"

She rose and opened her eyes to glare at him. "Not without you."

Anger and fear battled for control of his expression. "You need to leave, Reva. Now! Before—"

"I'm not leaving you, Jareth." She tore at the knots with trembling fingers. If she could just untie him…

"Reva, please go." Jareth's voice shook. "Better for me to die than you. I have three sisters to take my place—and you'll help them, I know you will. But your kingdom only has you. *Please, go!*"

"No!" The knots would not surrender to her bare fingers. Not only were they tied tightly, but the rain had made the ropes hard and slick, virtually impossible to untie. "Stop telling me what to do!"

"Reva—"

"I need to know something, Jareth," she said as she scraped her nails against the unyielding knots. "What I feel for you—and you for me. Is that just magic?"

Thunder crackled in the distance. She lifted her head to stare into the sea elf's face, searching for the answers she needed.

Something flickered in his eyes, the pain and hope and despair mingled into one tumultuous emotion.

"Is it?" she pressed.

His lips parted as rain dripped over his high cheekbones and down his stubbled jaw. "No," he said, the word a guttural cry. "No, it's not. The siren kiss bound you to the sea—not to my heart. Magic can't make you love, Reva. That's—that's you."

Relief expanded inside her. Reva's heart jumped in her chest, and then immediately began to ache. If only they had more time to explore what *this* meant, what it could be.

"Reva, you need to go—"

She leaned forward and pressed her mouth hard against Jareth's, silencing him with a kiss.

There was no magic in her kiss, no power to bind or save—only her heart, her hopes, her regrets. Rain and tears ran together down her cheeks as she said goodbye to the only person she could ever imagine ruling alongside her.

When she pulled back, she whispered desperately, "Whatever happens, I want you to know that I love you, Jareth Elesti, and I think you would have made a wonderful king for my people."

The surprise on Jareth's face transformed to horror. "Reva, no—"

A thundering roar cut him off and assaulted her ears, ten times louder this time. She twisted, horrified, toward the shadow kraken. Its monstrous shiny eyes hovered only a few dozen yards above them, its toothy maw gaping wide as it roared. It was staring straight at her.

Shaking, Reva dug in her pocket and yanked out Cassandra's pearl. By the sands, how did it work? She lifted the pearl toward the beast.

"I have your pearl!" she shouted into the monstrous face looming over her. "I order you to leave my island and never come back!"

The kraken's colossal mouth merely howled back at her wordlessly. Its face was larger than the entire side of the castle, its mouth displaying rows of sharp teeth. She placed herself squarely in front of Jareth and held the pearl high for the beast to see.

She longed to twist and look at Jareth once more, but there wasn't time. What had Cassandra said, that only a blood sacrifice would sate the beast?

Well, let it be her blood and no one else's.

Screaming, Reva launched herself straight toward the kraken descending on them. Behind her, Jareth yelled, but she focused on her boots against the stone beneath her feet, on the monster born of her stepmother's hatred and greed.

At the end of the battlement, she leaped onto the wide railing and launched herself into the open air, straight toward the kraken's mouth.

Rain slicked over her body as Reva catapulted into the kraken's mouth. She braced herself for pain as all light vanished. Darkness engulfed her. She squeezed her eyes shut, not wanting to watch as teeth tore her apart.

It was more likely she'd be swallowed whole and suffocate in the stomach of the monster.

For a horrific moment, Reva's world became nothing but darkness, heat, and the stench of death. Nothing else remained. Only blackness and decay.

She waited for the end and prayed to the seas that Cassandra was right about this blood sacrifice.

CHAPTER EIGHTEEN

Something screamed—not the guttural roar of a kraken, but something older. Tingles of pain shot up Reva's arm from the pearl she still clutched in her fingers. Thoughts forced their way into her head, terrible, nightmarish thoughts.

From the kraken?

No! The new voice screamed in her head.

The pearl grew colder, so cold her fingers froze to the smooth surface, and she couldn't drop it. Icy, burning pain leached into her skin. She flinched away from the horrific thoughts planted in her mind, not by the kraken but by the *pearl*—she saw people dying in the worst ways—fires burning, kingdoms crumbling, darkness simmering beneath the surface of Rhuin…and in the deep places of the sea.

She saw Etthan sinking beneath the frothing waves of the South Oloren. Her lips parted in a scream, but no sound escaped her. She couldn't let this happen—this couldn't be their fate.

But the images continued to pummel her thoughts, and she wondered: Were these foretellings of the future? Or images from ages long ago? Or some strange, twisted combination of both past and future?

Then the nightmarish visions shifted. She saw herself suspended above the castle, body arched backward with pain, her arms strung to the side as if she were the sacrifice bound between two pillars.

For Etthan, she thought as a shaft of light cut through her body.

For Jareth.

Hot white light replaced the darkness. The evil within the pearl emitted one final wail as a shockwave slammed into Reva's body, flinging her backward. She screamed as rain and seawater exploded around her, pounding against her with agonizing force. When she opened her eyes, gray sky and writhing shadows swirled everywhere.

Then her body slammed into something firm that deflected her momentum and tumbled her against unyielding stone. Pain pummeled her body as she rolled against a stone pillar.

Biting back tears, knowing she had to get up and face the kraken again, Reva opened her eyes.

But the kraken looming over Etthan curled in on itself like smoke above a fire, only to fade into tendrils that blew away in the storm's stiff wind.

And then, as if the storm itself had been born of vile magic, the rain dissipated, the clouds parted, and a shaft of light spilled across the battlement, shining on her face. Reva squinted into the brightness, unable to move or breathe or think.

Then a shadow came between her and the sunlight and a hand settled on her shoulder. "Your Highness! Are you alright?"

She blinked as a face came into focus. Rency leaned over her, grinning like a fool. She allowed him to pull her into a seated position.

"You slayed the beast, you darling girl!" He waved a hand toward the place the kraken had once been. "I've never seen anything like it—the way you—the way you—I can't believe you did that for me. I would have been squished like a bug by that vile monster. I knew you cared."

When he winked at her, Reva groaned. "Didn't do—for you—" She waved him away and drew in a shuddering breath. "Go away—I need to catch—my breath."

"Reva!" Jareth called her name, twisting his head to look over his shoulder. "Are you hurt?"

She shook her head, gulping in huge mouthfuls of air. Considering the fact she hurt pretty much *everywhere,* Reva knew she'd sustained injuries, but when she tested her arms and legs, everything moved like it should.

Reva stilled, however, when she noticed the black substance coating her skin and clothing. Kraken blood?

She wiped at the front of her tunic with her free hand with no success.

"Here." Crouching beside her, Rency fished a handkerchief from his pocket and grabbed her chin firmly. She squirmed as he roughly wiped her face.

"That better have been a clean handkerchief," she muttered when he finally released her.

He smirked and reached for her hand, the one still clutching the death pearl. Reva growled his name.

The pirate's gaze flew to hers, his fingers hovering just over hers.

"Touch that pearl, and you'll be steering the *Andromeda* with a hook for a hand," she warned in a low voice.

The corner of his mouth lifted, but something shifted in his eyes—a subtle darkening that made her body stiffen in preparation for a fight. But then he grinned and patted her on the head.

"Wouldn't dream of it, love," he said, rocking back on his heels. "I'm no petty thief."

"Of course not. You're a *pirate*."

He shrugged and didn't seem remotely offended. "Semantics."

Reva snorted and jammed the pearl deep into her pocket. Later, she'd figure out the proper way to destroy and dispose of a Death Pearl. For now, she planned to keep it on her person at all times.

Groaning as pain rippled through every muscle in her abused body, she braced her palm against the ground and tried to make her weak legs shift beneath her. Rency caught her by the elbow and hauled her to her feet. With one hand on her arm and the other on her hip, he maneuvered her so she could lean against the pillar. Reva blinked away the stars spackling her vision and shoved him away.

"Can someone untie me now?"

Jareth's plaintive request brought a smile to Reva's mouth.

"Rency, would you do the honors?" she asked. "I seem to have lost my—"

"Reva!" Felix's annoyingly familiar voice cut her off.

She groaned and turned as the Destan prince strode across the battlement, waving a sword in one hand. Reva's soldiers clustered behind him, looking confused and disheveled. "I was coming to help," Felix said, "but I see you've already vanquished the monster."

"Right." She eyed him, without an ounce of belief. "Thank you for your...*courageous intentions.*"

Felix nodded grimly, either not noticing her sarcasm or not caring.

Reva then turned her attention to her men. They formed themselves into an uneven line, expressions ranging from confusion to embarrassment to something hung between the two. "Who's in charge?" she asked.

One of the older soldiers took a step forward. "Lamont, but he—he's gone, Your Highness." He cleared his throat and studied the ground. Then, he stiffened his spine and lifted his head, staring straight ahead. "I think that means I am, Your Highness."

"Very well." Reva clutched at her stomach, suppressing the surge of guilt and sorrow that threatened to undo her. How many of her people had she lost today? "I want you and your men to go to the regent's chambers and place her under arrest."

The man's gaze flew to hers, uncertain. "Your—Your Highness?"

"The charge is treason. And murder. And a slew of other things I'll have my counselors draft up later. Just get her in irons, and we'll sort out the details soon."

The guard hesitated but then pounded his fist against his chest, in a salute. After barking orders to the rest of the soldiers, he led the way from the battlement.

Arms reached around her from behind. Reva jerked, twisting to defend herself, but Jareth's face loomed briefly over hers before he tugged her against his chest. She let him, and it felt good. Really good. He buried his face in the hollow of her shoulder, body trembling as held her against his chest.

Her heart stuttered as she awkwardly patted his back.

"Don't ever do anything like that again," he whispered into her hair, voice thick with emotion. "You're going to be the death of me, Reva."

She laughed despite herself. "Well, at least you're fully aware of what you're getting yourself into."

"Sand and sharks," Rency said from behind her. "What an exhausting day. I could use a hug too, Reva."

Jareth growled something and lifted his head. Reva took great pleasure in imagining the foul look the elf prince might be throwing toward the pirate captain just then.

"Right. No hugs for poor, poor me." Rency sighed dramatically.

Reva pulled away from Jareth and turned as Felix cleared his throat. "Speaking of poor, poor you," Felix said, stepping closer to Reva. "Are you going to honor our agreement?"

"Of course." She forced the words past stiff lips as Jareth's hand trailed down over her wrist to grip her hand. "I'm a woman of my word. I keep my promises."

Jareth's hand flexed and tightened.

Reva turned her attention to Rency, who lounged against the pillar with arms crossed over his damp tunic. "Rency," she said in her coldest tone, "you stand accused of treason and kidnapping."

The pirate captain's mouth slackened, and he drew himself stiffly to attention. "Wait—what?"

"How do you plead?"

Rency's sun-weathered skin took on a sickly hue. "Now, Reva—"

"Rency." She cut him off with a swipe of the hand. "I'm going to give you *one* chance to redeem yourself. You claim you're not a pirate, so it's time you proved it."

His eyes narrowed. "And how do you propose I do that?"

Felix cleared his throat again but—for once—kept his mouth shut and let Reva do the talking.

"I am requisitioning the *Andromeda* for a special rescue mission."

Rency's eyes pulled into even tighter slits. "And who, pray tell, will I be rescuing?"

"Felicity." Felix said the name as if it were a prayer.

Reva pursed her lips to suppress a smile at the lovesick tone in the prince's voice. "She's been sold into slavery by an unscrupulous person who shall remain unmentioned. All you need to know is that your duty is to find and rescue this young woman. And when you do—if you do—I'll sign a royal pardon and *not* hang you."

"Now, Reva, I don't really have time to rescue more damsels in distress. I have a business to run, you know."

"No, you'd prefer to kidnap the young ladies instead, I'm sure," Reva said around a heavy sigh. For once, couldn't he be the honorable person she hoped might lurk deep, deep—very deep—inside? "This girl needs your help. Is it so much to ask you to set aside your pirating for a few months to bring her home? In exchange for *not being hanged?*"

"Can't we just hang him?" Jareth whispered under his breath. "I prefer that plan, honestly."

Reva shot him an amused look. "I'm sure you do, but poor Felicity would prefer to be rescued, I think. I realize that you and Rency seem to be confused on this point, but girls generally prefer freedom over imprisonment. We don't usually find kidnapping enjoyable."

Jareth's cheeks reddened, and he avoided her gaze.

"Well?" Felix demanded, one hand on his hip, the other holding onto his sword as if he had no idea what to do with it. "Are you going to do it or not?"

Rency didn't answer immediately. He made them wait and—judging by the smirk tugging at his mouth—enjoyed it. "Very well," he finally said, tossing his hands up as if he'd lost all patience with the lot of them. "I'll be the bigger person and rescue the poor, enslaved maiden."

"Excellent!" For the first time, Felix offered a genuine smile. "When do we leave?"

Horror clawed at Rency's expression. "I beg your pardon…*we?*"

"Oh, yes, didn't I mention that you'll be taking Felix with you?" Reva asked casually, unable to suppress the satisfied smile tugging at her mouth. The adrenaline of the battle and the exhilaration of *surviving* made everything seem *hilarious* right now. She felt like she could throw back her head and laugh for no reason. And then cry herself to sleep.

She wished she could be a fly on *Andromeda*'s hull so that she could enjoy every minute of the upcoming rescue mission. Rency deserved every minute of torture Felix would inflict upon him during their long, long, hopefully *very* long excursion.

The pirate captain looked ready to burst out of the few buttons holding his shirt onto his torso, but before he could argue, footsteps pounded against the battlement behind them. Reva turned to see her new captain of the guard rushing toward her.

"I'm sorry to interrupt, Your Highness," he said around labored breaths. "But we can't find the regent. She's disappeared."

Anxiety replaced the heady exhilaration Reva had been experiencing since defeating the kraken. "What do you mean? I left her on the balcony…" She ran to the edge of the battlement and peered down toward Cassandra's rooms far below. But the balcony was, indeed, empty.

From this distance, Reva couldn't even see the blood spatters that might be the only remaining evidence of the fight between her and her stepmother a few minutes earlier.

Her stomach tightened and a chill prickled over her skin. "Search the entire castle—the entire island, if need be," she said hoarsely. "I want her found."

"Yes, Your Highness." The guard's footsteps clomped away as he left to do her bidding.

Reva pressed her trembling hands against the stone railing and forced herself to inhale slow, deep breaths. They would find Cassandra.

They *had* to find her, because she was far too dangerous to be left on the loose.

CHAPTER NINETEEN

Reva felt sick, her emotions too frayed and battered to handle another shock like this one. The last thing she needed was a vengeful stepmother on the loose, causing havoc wherever she went.

"You may not find her." Rency's quiet voice tugged her out of her private fears. "It's possible that Cassandra's life was bound to the pearl, to the dark magic, to the kraken. And when you destroyed the monster and broke its power…"

"Oh." The idea sobered Reva, sending new shards of regret into her heart. As much as she despised her stepmother, she hadn't wanted her to *die*. "I'd not thought of that."

"Whatever the case, we can simply be glad she is gone," Jareth said. "That foul woman caused much pain and suffering."

Reva wasn't sure she dared believe Rency's theory. It would be a neat and tidy way to tie off the problem…but what if Cassandra hadn't died? What if she'd escaped?

Forcing herself to inhale a stabilizing breath, Reva tried to let the matter go. Her men would search for Cassandra, and if there was anything to find—they'd bring her back to stand trial for her crimes.

Instead, Reva forced her mind back to more pressing matters, ones within her control. How many people had been lost in the attack? The castle below had taken a tremendous beating. Parapets were smashed, leaving balconies half crushed and dangerously exposed. On the south side of the castle, an entire tower had disappeared. All that remained was a huge mound of stone smeared black with kraken blood.

And beyond that, the ships in the cove hadn't escaped unscathed either. At least two ships burned, casting dark plumes of smoke into the early morning sky. She was relieved to see that both the *Perseus* and *Andromeda* had survived and that both ships now drew close to the burning ones, presumably to offer aid.

Isla was out there, no doubt, barking orders and preparing to haul the injured on board.

Fingers lightly touched the back of Reva's hand. She glimpsed Jareth through her peripheral vision but didn't turn toward him. "You saved your people," he said quietly. "I don't know how you did it but focus on that. You saved as many as you could."

How did he know what she'd been thinking about?

"As the captain of the only sentient ship in these waters," Rency said loftily as he leaned against the battlement on Reva's other side, "and an expert on all things magical, I've deduced that the princess' willingness to sacrifice herself to the shadow beast in order to save everyone on the island is what broke the spell and slayed the monster. Unless she possesses some hidden magical talent that she hasn't shared with us…I'm guessing it was the sacrificial nature of her actions that did the trick."

"You think so?" Reva asked. Her thoughts on this matter would probably weigh heavily on her mind for many months to come. "Cassandra did say a blood sacrifice was required…so I suppose it is possible that the *willingness* to make a blood sacrifice might have accomplished the same thing instead."

"Yes, yes," Rency said, turning to lean his hip against the wall so that he could study her. "Everyone knows curses are broken by sacrifices and kissing."

Reva choked. *"Kissing?"*

"Haven't you heard of true love's kiss? In fact, if we want to make sure the kraken is good and properly defeated, maybe we should test it out with some kissing. Just to be safe."

On her other side, Jareth sidled closer so that he nearly brushed up against her. "If we need to test that the beast has well and truly departed, I will happily throw you from the battlements as a second blood sacrifice, Captain," he said, voice low and warning. "Very willingly."

"Oh, please." Rency waved a dismissing hand, although he still smirked. "I didn't mean *me*. I know when I am a beaten man. I just hope *Felix* appreciates his good fortune."

At this jibe, Reva's mood improved dramatically, but not for the reasons Rency may have intended. "Actually—"

"I *do* appreciate my good fortune," Felix said from behind them, "in having escaped marriage to the princess. No offense, Reva, I'm sure we would have made it work, but…"

"Your heart lies elsewhere," Reva said for him, half-smiling. What sort of girl Felicity must be to actually love this cowardly fellow? She couldn't even imagine. "As does mine."

Silence descended among them as the wind whipped across the battlement, driving the clouds to the south and leaving golden sunshine in their wake.

"What is he talking about?" Jareth asked quietly, shifting to settle his hand alongside Reva's on the battlement. "His heart lies elsewhere?"

Rency leaned closer as well. "Yes, indeed. Do tell what you and this nincompoop have been scheming in our absence. I feel left out."

"I say—"

But Rency shushed Felix with another wave of his hand. Reva turned her back on the pirate and faced Jareth instead, nerves fluttering in her stomach.

"Well, Felix and I were talking before the battle with the kraken," she began slowly. "He agreed to give me money for food in exchange for finding Felicity—"

"Which I am going to be doing," Rency interrupted, "so why am I not getting paid?"

"*You are not getting hung,*" Reva fired over her shoulder, silencing him with a warning look.

Rency wisely clamped his mouth closed.

She turned back to Jareth. "And now that I have the Death Pearl, it's entirely plausible that the blight in Etthan may…go away. If Etthan is under a curse—under Cassandra's curse—as Rency suggested the other day, then the crops might begin to grow again. And if the crops grow…"

"Then you don't need trade routes," Jareth said quietly.

She suppressed a smile, forcing her expression to remain neutral, queenly. "And if I don't need trade routes…"

Jareth's mouth broke into a smile that grew wider by the minute. "Then you don't need Felix," he said.

"I say," Felix grumbled again.

"Which means," Reva said with a dramatic sigh, "that I'm suddenly in need of a suitable…well…*suitor.*"

"I volunteer," Rency said in her ear, but the laughter in his voice told her otherwise. Honestly, the pirate—*merchant sailor*—was a brat, and she was almost certain he had never possessed any true interest in her.

Jareth shot Rency a foul look before grabbing Reva's hand in both of his. She searched his eyes. What she wouldn't give for a few moments alone with him—even if it meant having to throw Rency and Felix *both* from the battlement. There was so much she wanted to say—so much she wanted to hear *him* say.

Jareth seemed to share her thoughts, because he said nothing. He just looked at her through piercing sea-green eyes and made her want to stand there forever and memorize the facets of his irises and the emotions behind those windows to his soul.

"Well, let me be the first to congratulate you on a blissful betrothal," Rency said, breaking the moment.

Reva stiffened and rolled her eyes toward the skies. "Sands and pearls, Rency, he hasn't proposed, and I haven't accepted."

"But he's going to, and you will." Rency winked at her and darted forward to peck a kiss against her cheek. "So, congratulations. I can't hang around for the festivities. It seems I have a prior engagement with slavers. Ready, Felix?"

The prince of Desta stirred abruptly and looked startled. "I'm sorry…*now?*"

"Yes, now. What, you want to have a lovely cup of tea first?"

Color infused Felix's cheeks. "No," he said stiffly. "I'm ready."

"We'll escort you down to the beach," Reva said as she pulled away from Jareth. A sense of loss filled her as his fingers slipped from hers, but she steeled herself against it. Before she could devote herself to spending time with him, she needed to uphold her agreement and care for her people.

There would be time for proposals and kissing later.

"I want to make sure you actually leave my island," Reva continued as they headed toward the stairs littered with debris from the battlements above them.

"Your lack of faith in me is astounding." Rency fell into step behind her, the others at his heels.

"What faith?" she tossed over her shoulder.

They took the outer staircase around the north side of the castle until it settled onto the beach where she and Jareth had emerged from the sea not that long ago. Several of Rency's sailors waited beside a dinghy. They snapped to attention when they saw their captain striding across the sand.

"Prepare to cast off, mates!" Rency called as he strode past Reva. "We've a damsel to save, and a noose to escape!"

The sailors burst into chaotic motion, half of them leaping into the dinghy while the other half tried— less than successfully—to shove it out of the shallow waters.

Rency spun and swept Reva into a quick hug. To her relief, he didn't linger but plopped her back into the sand and took a quick step back, an angelic look on his face. "Goodbye, dear girl. It's been…something. I would say pleasant, but I don't think that's the word I'm looking for."

Then he splashed through the shallows to stand waist deep in the water beside the bobbing dinghy. "Coming, Felix?"

Felix strode after him, muttering under his breath. Reva smothered a smile with her hand as the pirates dragged him unceremoniously into the boat.

Still in the water, Rency lifted a hand in farewell, but his shout of goodbye transformed into an inhuman shriek. He released the boat, thrashing both hands down into the water. A moment later, his fingers reappeared holding a pink blob with eight tentacles.

"Oy, Jareth!" he bawled. "One of your krakens just bit my   "

He yelped again and splashed through the water to pull another baby from the waves. Reva burst into loud laughter as Jareth dove forward. He caught the kraken babies that Rency tossed, none too gently, toward him. With a black look in their direction, Rency hastily boarded his dinghy, one hand pressed against his backside.

Jareth splashed back to the beach, holding Calix and another baby in his hands. "I didn't know they'd escaped," he mumbled, grinning at Reva.

"Poor hungry babies," Reva said as leaned down to pat them both on their pink heads, "and nothing to eat but dirty pirate, too. I'll get you something decent to eat…how does some nice slimy seaweed sound? Or do you prefer fish?"

"They aren't picky at this age." Jareth's smile widened as she straightened to look him in the eye. An awkward silence fell between them, now that they were suddenly alone.

At last, Jareth cleared his throat and took a step closer. "About what Rency said earlier…about me proposing…am I allowed to do so now? You are the only woman, above the sea or under, in this kingdom or any other, with whom I wish to share my life. I've never seen your like for bravery, for kindness."

As he spoke, the words flew faster and faster from his mouth, as if he were trying to get them all out before he lost his nerve.

Reva smiled and reached up to stroke the elf's cheek.

"Of course you may propose," she said with a mischievous smile. "And I will probably accept. After I've bathed and put on clean clothes. I smell like kraken. No offense."

"None taken." The anxiety eased from Jareth's face at her words, replaced instead with something bright and hopeful.

"We also need to discuss how to move your people from Argos," Reva said, the humor draining from her voice.

"I believe you'll agree that this should be done as soon as possible. Although, until I receive funds from Felix…we're going to be eating a lot of seafood."

"We can help with that," Jareth answered without hesitation.

"I'm hoping our people can learn to get along like we have. Peaceably." Her thoughts strayed back to Cassandra, and the battle at sea that had cost the lives of her parents and probably a large number of other souls on both sides.

"Peaceably?" Jareth took another step closer, leaning down to smile into her upturned face. "I would prefer *happily*."

"Happily ever after?" Reva leaned up on her toes, her gaze shifting to his mouth.

"I *do* like the sound of that." He pursed his lips briefly. "Reva, may I-I mean—would it be alright if—if—"

"Please, just kiss me," she whispered back.

With the baby krakens cradled between them, Jareth closed the distance and pressed his mouth over hers. Reva's heart skittered wildly, and she forced herself to remember her manners and kept her hands to herself.

There were babies watching after all.

And to think, she had found both love and salvation for her people all because of Cassandra's obsession with power and her evil death pearl. Reva gave into temptation and lifted her hand to stroke her fingers through Jareth's long, dark hair…

Reva's eyes popped open, and she cried out against Jareth's mouth.

"The pearl!" she gasped.

His darkened eyes seemed to struggle focusing on her as he pulled back. "What?"

Her hand moved to the pocket in her trousers, a pocket that felt suspiciously…

Empty.

"Oh, no," she rasped as her fingers dug through an empty pocket. "No, no, no."

"Let me look," Jareth offered. He shoved Calix and the other kraken into her hands and began to dig through his *own* pockets. Her eyebrows rose as he pulled a bracelet out and then a signet ring. These too he thrust into her hands.

His cheeks had gone as red as a blazing sunset. "It's the krakens, you see," he mumbled as he retrieved a necklace with an emerald set in a gold casing, and then a small box that was all too familiar. "Would you believe these fellows are the worst of thieves?"

"Those are my earrings!"

"I'm sorry. I truly intended to return everything, but I didn't want anyone to think I was the one stealing. I was afraid they'd hang me just for being an elf." Jareth regarded her sheepishly.

Reva's lips firmed as she shook her head. "Perhaps," she said wryly, "you can find my missing dagger, as well."

"You mean this?"

The dagger appeared from a deep pocket at the bottom of his vest, a kraken clinging to the hilt with all eight arms.

"Yes, that. Now the pearl?"

He searched the rest of his pockets, but Reva's flickering hopes vanished when he produced no pearl.

"As happy as I am to have my possessions back, I need the pearl, Jareth," Reva said, accepting the dagger and earrings from the tiny pink thieves.

"I have another pocket to search," he mumbled, continuing to dig. He withdrew a golden chain with a pocket watch dangling on the end.

Now who had recently complained about a missing watch…

Blistering sands and pearls!

"Rency," she gasped.

She should have known he'd try something like this to make sure he got paid. When had he stolen the pearl, when he leaned her up against the pillar? When he'd hugged her here on the beach? Some other cleverly concealed moment when he'd distracted her while picking her pocket?

Jareth's searching hands fell still, and his gaze shot to the sea beyond Reva.

"That thieving scoundrel!" she snarled. She thrust the krakens and all their stolen plunder back at Jareth and spun, dashing to the waterline and plowing into the waves. "Rency!" she shouted to the pirate dingy bouncing across the water. "You thieving liar! I know what you did! Get your deceitful, pilfering carcass back on this beach!"

Rency's laughter echoed across the sea. He stood from his place in the back of the boat and waved merrily to her. "Afraid I can't do that!" he shouted back. "It seems I have a maiden to rescue from slavery! And you know me—I can't resist the gallant side of my nature!"

Then, he reached into the pocket of his greatcoat and drew out a shiny black pearl, which he waved grandly in the air.

"Many thanks, Reva!" he shouted to her. "I vow to keep it safe and use it wisely."

"*Rency!*"

"Farewell, Princess Reva! Live long and happily with your elven prince, and I shall do the same with my plundered treasure!"

He kissed the pearl soundly before stowing it back in his pocket. Then he blew her a kiss as well before turning his back and waving wildly to his crew, who began to row with renewed vigor.

"Oh, that man!" Reva snarled, thigh deep in the water. "He's going to get himself killed if that thing still works—and who knows how many other people?"

Could she swim fast enough to catch up with him? Jareth waded in beside her, still trying to stuff Calix's plunder back into various pockets.

"Are you thinking what I'm thinking?" Reva asked him, pointing toward the escaping pirate dinghy.

Jareth successfully stuffed the last item into his vest and reached to grab her hand in his. "That you'd like a necklace made of pirate teeth?"

"That's exactly what I'm thinking. Are any of your big krakens about?"

Jareth flashed her a devilish smile. "What do you think?"

"Well, call them. Call them *all*." Reva waded deeper into the water as Jareth caught her hand and tugged her alongside him.

"Am I allowed to breathe for you?" he asked. "If we're going swimming, you're going to need to breathe, you know."

Reva wasn't sure if she should laugh or smack him for his impertinence. "Of course you can breathe for me. I'll give you all the kisses you want if you just get me to that sands-blighted boat!" She jabbed a finger toward Rency's dinghy as it plowed wildly toward the *Andromeda*.

Jareth lifted her hand and kissed her damp fingertips. "Aye, aye, my lady," he said with a wink.

Then he wrapped her in his arms and plunged them both beneath the aquamarine waves.

Rency (and the Andromeda*) will return one day with more pirates, pearls, and plunder…*

Pearls of Salt and Sacrifice *is book 2 in the* Sacrificed Hearts *multi-author series, a collection of stand-alone fantasy romances inspired by monsters of legend, each tale packed with strong heroines, swoony heroes, and sacrificial themes. Read the next adventure in* Mask of Deception and Sacrifice *by Callie Thomas.*

DON'T MISS THE NEXT BOOK!

If she can remove the monster's mask, she will earn her freedom…but failure will cost her life.

Thirteen years ago, Princess Fiona fled the bloodshed within Ravenwood Castle. She has no desire to return to the place of her childhood nightmares, especially not as a prisoner locked in chains. Using the power of illusion, she glamours her appearance to conceal her royal identity, hoping that her facade won't crumble before she can escape.

When the usurper king forces her on a deadly mission to subdue a wild man terrorizing his kingdom, Fiona must earn the trust of a masked monster who uses his sharp tongue and shifting personalities to keep her away. But the longer she's with him, the more she sees beyond his disguise and succumbs to his charms.

With her life on the line, the last thing she needs is a distraction. But when he offers her another path to freedom, will she sacrifice everything for him?

Loosely inspired by the gothic romance of Phantom of the Opera *and* Jane Eyre*, this spooky romantasy features hidden*

MORE FROM
EVERLY HAYWOOD

BETWEEN SHADE AND FLAME SERIES

Peaceweaver
Grimkeeper
Runemaster
Songbender
Seastormer (Coming Soon)

identities, forbidden magic, and scarred pasts—perfect for fans of Stephanie Garber and Shari L. Tapscott! Mask of Deception and Sacrifice *is book 3 in the* Sacrificed Hearts *multi-author series, a collection of stand-alone fantasy romances inspired by monsters of legend and packed with strong heroines, swoony heroes, and sacrificial themes.*

Find the book on Amazon today!

ABOUT THE AUTHOR

EVERLY HAYWOOD imagines herself to be a shieldmaiden of great prowess…but you're more likely to find her in a dusty library. She writes swoony-sweet romantic fantasy about strong leading ladies and brooding but huggable heroes. An advocate for her Goblin Princess with Down Syndrome, she also features characters with disabilities. When she isn't tangled up in magical curses or drinking pumpkin spice coffee, she can be found weeding her garden, homeschooling her Fairy Princess, and reading books by authors like Maggie Stiefvater, Elise Kova, and Sylvia Mercedes.

Sign up for her newsletter today to receive a free book!

www.everlyhaywood.com/newsletter/